A QUIET ROOM IN HELL

When Mike Faraday, the laconic L.A. private investigator, is asked by lawyer Andrew Dillon to tail the scientist Dr Hugo Greenbach, he is soon plunged into murder and mayhem up to his eyeballs. For Greenbach had stumbled on a formula which a lot of people were after, including a powerful Chinese Triad organisation. The problems are only finally resolved after a murderous shoot-out in a deserted house as Mike finds a new use for TV channels.

BASIL COPPER

A QUIET ROOM IN HELL

Complete and Unabridged

LINFORD
Leicester

First published in Great Britain

First Linford Edition
published 1998

British Library CIP Data

Copper, Basil, *1924*–
   A quiet room in hell.—Large print ed.—
Linford mystery library
1. Detective and mystery stories
2. Large type books
I. Title
823.9′14 [F]

ISBN 0–7089–5294–1

Published by
F. A. Thorpe (Publishing) Ltd.
Anstey, Leicestershire

Set by Words & Graphics Ltd.
Anstey, Leicestershire
Printed and bound in Great Britain by
T. J. International Ltd., Padstow, Cornwall

This book is printed on acid-free paper

1

I crossed the lobby and rode up in the elevator to the third floor of the Schuyler Building. It was raining this morning and the rain and the smog together made a nice blur of the L.A. landscape. Droplets of water ran down my hair, off the top of my raincoat and made rivulets down my back. It was Monday morning too. The world is sure beating hell out of you, Faraday, I told myself.

There was a girl in the elevator as well as the operator. She was a nice-looking girl with fine breasts, in a blue linen shirt and with pale blue slacks that emphasized the boyish slimness of her figure. She had dark lacquered hair and discreet pink finger-nails that one longed to have fondling one's ear. She looked me up and down pretty snootily but I could see what she was thinking and presently she broke out in a smile that was about 9.5 millimetres wide. She had white teeth too and everything else to go with them. I figured she must work in the building because there wasn't a drop of moisture on her anywhere.

She got off at the second floor, unfortunately, where a major oil company had its local offices. She was probably the managing director's private secretary. Or something about that price range.

"Terrible morning, Miss Popkiss," the elevator-boy said.

He was a melancholy-looking character of about sixty-five, with silvered hair that looked like an old toilet brush that had seen better days.

The girl looked at me sympathetically.

"It can't always be sunshine, Harold," she told the elevator-boy.

"You can say that again, Miss Popkiss," I said.

The dark job looked liked someone was burning old linoleum under her nostrils but her façade was only dented, not cracked.

"It can't always be sunshine," she said.

"Thanks for the recording," I said.

"My name's Mike Faraday. I'm in the book."

Miss Popkiss gave me a dazzling smile.

"The figures make my eyes ache, Mr Farragut," she said sweetly as the elevator door slid shut.

The elevator-man gave me an all-time loser's smile.

"I know," I told him before he could open his mouth. "You can't win them all. And it is Monday."

"Miss Popkiss is a very nice girl," he said defensively.

"Don't rub it in," I told him.

I got out at the third and went down the teak-panelled corridor with the concealed lighting looking for Andrew Dillon's office. He was a lawyer with a practice in this building and he'd asked to see me.

The pecking of typewriters came from behind the closed doors and with it the expensive aroma of Havana cigars. I could smell money here from the thick carpeting in the corridor to the tasteful water colour originals in the anodised metal frames that hung on the walls.

I only hoped some of it would rub off on me.

I found Dillon's place in the end and walked on in like it said in black letters on the frosted glass door. It was a nice lay-out. The room was slightly smaller than the passenger lounge of the QE2 and appeared to be floored in wall-to-wall mink. There were a few genuine oils hung on the tasteful cream walls, each of them with a small strip-light beneath.

There was a railed enclosure; a couple of teak desks; some filing cabinets; a water cooler and a genuine eighteenth-century map of the Massachusetts area in an oak frame. I figured my fee was safe whatever the outcome of the case. A fair-haired girl in a cream linen suit was sitting at a desk outside the railed enclosure, buffing her nails and looking like she was too important to notice my presence. She had a scarlet silk scarf around her brown throat.

The scarf was tucked into the lapels of her suit and held in place with a little leather cylinder like boy scouts used to wear. I figured she might have been a

Brownie denmother in her spare time. When I got up closer and noticed her figure I realized it was unlikely. The stuff she'd got was too important to waste on young girls.

She went on buffing her nails like I didn't exist. I was used to that of course so I just smiled, and took off my raincoat and shook it out while I waited. The girl's cool eyes didn't register my presence by so much as a flicker.

"When you've finished re-arranging your cuticles you might tell Dillon Mike Faraday is here," I said.

The blonde number held out one of her finger-nails like it was a Rubens study from his late period and ran a pink tongue over very white teeth.

"I might," she told the filing cabinets.

She gave me a supercilious look from steady grey eyes.

"Please yourself," I said. "I'm perfectly happy here, I'm on retainer and expenses plus per day and Dillon's picking up the tab."

The girl flickered her long eye-lashes

and went on admiring her finger-nails.

"I could tell you were Faraday as soon as you came in," she said. "You're certainly no gentleman."

"Dillon doesn't want a gentleman," I said. "They're no good for private-eye work. Besides which, they went out with the snood."

The blonde number gurgled to herself but the façade didn't quite crack. She reached out with her disengaged hand and picked up a red plastic phone.

"Mr Faraday to see you, Mr Dillon."

She smiled, her insolent eyes raking me over.

"Sure, Mr Dillon. I'll tell him."

She put the phone back in its cradle with a pink hand.

"He's working on some papers," she said. "It'll take about ten minutes."

"You got a name?" I said.

"Certainly," she said. "It's Della Strongman. And no puns about it. It's been done before."

"What's Dillon got on his mind?" I said.

The girl smiled for the first time,

looking directly at me. It was something to see.

"Same thing as you," she said sweetly. "But I've learned to keep him at his distance."

I gave her a long look.

"The assignment," I said.

"Oh, that."

The Strongman number finished fooling with her fingers and spread her arms across the desk. Her nails made ten bright splotches like drops of blood across the white of the blotter.

"He'll tell you when he sees you."

"Supposing you tell me?" I said.

The girl shook her head.

"It's more than my job's worth."

"And what is your job worth?" I said.

The girl looked at me with coolly appraising eyes.

"About half what I'm paid." she said.

"It's the way of the world," I told her.

Just then the phone buzzed again. The girl had it tight beneath her chin so fast the instrument made a dull blur in the air.

"Certainly, Mr Dillon."

She put the phone back.

"You can go in now."

I thanked her and went on over toward a polished teak door in the far corner of the room which had Andrew Dillon in gold curlicue letters on the panel. I turned back just before I went in. The girl was still sitting in the same position but I knew she could see me because she was looking rather too intently in the telephone mirror. I grinned as I opened the door and went on in.

★ ★ ★

Andrew Dillon was a tall, good-looking man of about forty-five, with a deep tan; an expensive haircut; and a generally sharp, well-groomed look. He had flinty grey eyes; strong white teeth in a rather fleshy mouth and a lean, rangy body in a blue yachting blazer with silver buttons. He either spent all his spare time on boats, fairways or beaches or he'd seen too many Cary Grant thirties movies. Either way he was a pretty impressive sight.

8

He sat back in a brown leather chair behind his black glass-top desk and waved a well-manicured thumb in my direction.

"Sit down, Mr Faraday. I won't keep you a moment. Just finishing off these figures."

"Sure," I said.

I sat down in the uncomfortable teak and chromed steel chair that he reserved for his clients and looked enviously at his own padded seat. The slats in the chair were making nice grooves in my butt already. Dillon picked up a Turkish cigarette from a crystal tray in front of him and blew a cloud of aromatic smoke over his desk, fumigating a couple of moths that were dancing a gavotte on one corner.

I sat and admired the decor for another couple of minutes. This was the bit meant to impress the clients and I guessed Dillon couldn't give up the act easily. He finished at last, closed his brown card folder with a contented sigh and put the tips of his fingers together on the blotter in front of him.

"Cigarette, Mr Faraday?"

I shook my head.

"I'll use my own, if you don't mind."

He shrugged.

"By all means."

He waited while I lit up and feathered smoke at the ceiling to compete with his own.

"I guess you're wondering why I called you out here?"

I shook my head.

"I gave up wondering in my business a long time ago, Mr Dillon."

Dillon smiled thinly. It was his court smile and there was little humour in it. I guessed he practised it in front of the mirror for hours. It was certainly effective with juries but it didn't do anything for me. But then I wasn't a client of Dillon's. Not in that sense, anyway.

Maybe he guessed what I was thinking because he turned it off. It seemed to kill his face momentarily. It was like a five hundred watt bulb going out. He stared at me suspiciously.

"You heard of a character called Dr Hugo Greenbach?"

I shook my head.

"Not until now. What's he supposed to have done?"

Dillon shook his head and shifted uneasily in his padded chair.

"Nothing, Mr Faraday," he said patiently. "He's a client of mine. I want him followed."

I looked at Dillon steadily for a moment.

"What do you mean, followed? I'm not too fond of tail-work."

Dillon shook his head again. Faint sparks of irritation were dancing in his grey eyes.

"You don't get the picture, Mr Faraday. It's nothing like that."

"Fill me in," I said.

Dillon put his well-manicured hands together on the blotter and stared at them gloomily.

"It's a complicated story, Mr Faraday."

"I've got plenty of time," I said.

Dillon controlled himself with an effort. He wasn't an easy man to dislike and I'd already got a head-start.

"To put it briefly, Mr Faraday, Dr

Greenbach's had some threats against his life."

I eased myself in the slatted chair and tortured a different part of my anatomy.

"You need a bodyguard, Mr Dillon. You can get plenty of those round L.A."

"I need you, Mr Faraday," Dillon said steadily. "That's why I sent for you."

There was an anguished yelp creeping into his syllables. I went on needling him. I was beginning to enjoy myself now. Despite the slatted chair.

"What am I supposed to do? Stop a bullet instead of Greenbach? And what's his racket?"

Dillon looked pained.

"Dr Greenbach's a most respected industrial chemist. I'm willing to pay a thousand bucks down, another thousand at the end of the assignment, plus your usual daily fee and expenses."

I stared at him for a long moment.

"You interest me, Mr Dillon."

Dillon blew out some more smoke from his perfumed cigarette. One of the moths had a sudden attack of palsy and staggered off the desk-edge.

"I thought I might, Mr Faraday," he said. "I take it you accept?"

"Not so fast," I said. "I'd like to know a little more about the assignment."

Dillon made like he hadn't heard. He was scribbling something on one of his business cards he took from a corner of the blotter.

"Here's his address. He's located on Laurel Canyon. Pick him up around six tonight. Miss Strongman will give you the thousand bucks on the way out. I'd like a receipt."

"Sure," I said. "Looks like you just hired me. I daresay Greenbach will fill me in on the details."

Dillon looked at me sharply.

"He's not to know anything about it," he said.

I looked moodily at Dillon.

"His life's in danger; I'm to tail him; he's not to know. Sounds like a great assignment."

Dillon smiled faintly.

"You want the money or not?"

I grinned.

"Do I like breathing?" I said.

13

Dillon relaxed.

"You'll pick things up as you go along," he said. "Just make sure Greenbach stays in one piece. Report to me once a week. And let me have your account at the same time. We'll pay by the week."

"Sounds like you think Greenbach may not last," I said.

Dillon shifted behind the desk again.

"He'll be all right with you behind him, Mr Faraday," he said comfortably.

I got up.

"Thanks for the Chinese riddles," I said.

I walked on over toward the door. I stopped and turned to face Dillon. At that distance he could have passed for Walter Pidgeon in M.G.M.'s plushiest days.

"Gun stuff?" I said.

Dillon nodded.

"Gun stuff." he said.

I smiled again.

"Just so long as we know."

I went on out to collect my thousand dollars.

2

"Sounds screwy to me, Mike," Stella said.

She looked at me quizzically. I sat back at my old broadtop and stared at the cracks in the ceiling.

"That's the name of the game, honey," I said. "What Faraday Investigations is all about."

Stella smiled. The afternoon sun spilled through the blinds and made deep bands of shadow across the office carpet. The plastic fan pecked at the edges of the silence, redistributing the tired air. Stella's face had wide bars of light and shadow across it. Down below the muffled roar of the stalled traffic on the boulevard made a faint protest through the smog and the scorched atmosphere.

With it came the elusive perfume that makes living in the L.A. basin such a delight to the inhabitants; a compound of tropical flowers and the stink of gasoline.

Combined with the roasting beans of a nearby coffee-shop it made a pretty potent mixture.

"Who is Dr Hugo Greenbach, Mike?"

I shrugged.

"I was hoping you'd tell me."

"It wouldn't take long to look him up," Stella said.

"After the coffee," I told her.

Stella got up. The sunlight spilling in at the top of the blind made a dazzling cone of her hair. She rat-tatted with very high heels over to the glassed-in alcove where we do the brewing-up. I sat and salivated like one of Pavlov's dogs as I heard the snick of the percolator going on.

Stella put her head round the screen.

"You should have asked Dillon for payment in coffee, Mike. Have you seen the price this week?"

I grinned.

"Never mind about the price, honey. We're temporarily in funds. Dillon shelled out a thousand bucks as a retainer. The same at the finish of the assignment, plus exes and daily fee."

Stella's blue eyes were wide as she came back toward me.

"The hell he did. Dr Greenbach must be an important character."

"Or Dillon's protecting an investment," I said.

"What's that supposed to mean?" Stella said.

I shrugged and shifted my position at the desk. Stella moved away warily like she knew what I was thinking. It was too hot for that sort of horsing around this afternoon anyway. I took out the bundle of greenbacks and passed them over to Stella.

"You'd better pay those into the account in the morning. And let Dillon have an official receipt."

Stella took the money and riffled it dreamily. It made an agreeably crisp noise.

"Will do," she said.

"No need to be so reverent," I said. "You've seen money before."

"True," Stella said. "But maybe I've been with Faraday Investigations too long."

17

I looked her in the eye.

"That'll be the day," I said.

She came toward me and laid a warm finger along the angle of jaw. I stood it for so long but she was well away before I made my move. I sat and watched her put the money in the safe behind the large-scale map of L.A. on the far wall. The safe could be opened with a reasonably sturdy toothpick but it makes us feel secure. Stella went back to the alcove and presently I could get the agreeable aroma of roasted beans. She came back and put the cup on my blotter, went back for her own.

There's nothing like the first cup. I added a mite more sugar and there was silence for a while as I did justice to it. Stella went over to sit at her own desk and looked at me thoughtfully. Today she wore pale blue linen slacks with a tan leather belt round the mid-riff and her open-neck scarlet silk shirt set off the brown pillars of her throat in a way I found disconcerting.

"So you're going out there at six?" she said.

"I took the job," I said. "Dillon said it might be gun-stuff."

I lowered another sip of coffee.

"You're taking the Smith-Wesson?"

I nodded.

"Too true I am. There's something doesn't sit right about this assignment."

"Dillon's able enough," Stella said. "One of the city's best criminal lawyers."

"I'm not denying that." I said. "But I get a gut-feeling when clients don't tell me the whole story."

Stella put her cup down with a faint clinking.

"You're exaggerating, Mike. He didn't tell you a damn thing. Period."

I avoided the wry look in her eyes. She had a point though. I went on smoking and listening to the traffic noises and avoiding Stella's eyes. She gave up in the end and went over to the small reference library she had established. She selected a massive tome and carried it back to her desk. I squinted across at the gold title on the blue binding but I couldn't make it out.

"Who's picking up the tab for that?" I said.

Stella looked up from her page riffling and grinned.

"Mr Memory," she said. "It was paid for years ago. Don't you remember?"

I shook my head. Stella looked faintly shocked.

"We've had it four-five years. We had quite an argument about it. In the end it's proved about the most useful reference work we ever got. It came off your income tax."

"That's all right then," I said.

I sat relishing Stella's expression and watched her go on thumbing pages. She stopped presently and started taking notes on her pad with her gold pencil. She turned back to me.

"Quite a brilliant character, Mike. Industrial chemist. Vice-President of one of our major chemical plants. Lot of scientific papers."

"You can skip those," I said. "The pronunciations only hurt my teeth."

Stella glanced at me happily and went on reading out loud.

"Unmarried. Pretty rich, I'd imagine. Two addresses here, apart from the Laurel Canyon house."

I frowned across at the neon-shimmer on the window.

"Anything there likely to explain why Dillon wants him watched?"

Stella shook her head.

"Nothing on the surface, Mike."

I shrugged, stubbing out my cigarette butt in the earthenware tray on my desk.

"It's about par for the course."

Stella sat tapping very white teeth with her gold pencil and saying nothing.

"Greenbach's a client of Dillon's," I said. "The old boy's had some threats against his life. So he must have confided in Dillon."

"You think a pretty good thought. Mike," Stella said admiringly. "You'll be putting Pascal out of business next."

I gave Stella what I hoped was a withering look but like always it didn't have any effect; just bounced off the armourplate.

"I haven't finished yet, honey," I said.

"Question is, did Greenbach ask for protection or not? If he didn't, then Dillon's disobeying orders."

"Natch," Stella said. "Because if he did Dillon would have no need to keep it secret."

"It's getting too complicated," I said. Stella shook her head, making a tangled frieze of gold about her eyes. She glanced at me pityingly.

"You always did have trouble keeping two ideas in your head at once, Mike."

I ignored that.

"Why would an industrial chemist, brilliant or otherwise, get threats against his life?" I said.

Stella gave me a dazzling look from her blue eyes.

"You're the detective, Mike. That's what you're supposed to find out."

"Maybe," I said moodily. "I'll just have to play it by ear."

Stella grinned.

"It wouldn't be the first time."

She got up without being asked and went to get me another cup of coffee. I reached into the drawer of my desk, got out the Smith-Wesson in the nylon holster. I took off my jacket, buckled the nylon harness on and replaced my jacket. I felt properly dressed then. By that time Stella was back. She put the coffee down and went over to her own desk.

I sat down and finished the coffee in silence. Stella sat watching me with that marvellous tact of hers. She sealed up the envelope in front of her and stacked the mail for the evening. It was a comfortable silence. I didn't break it. We'd sat here a lot of times like that when business was quiet. I often wondered what went on behind the smooth forehead and cool manner. I had a shrewd idea. I left off the speculation in the end. The weather was too hot and the topic too dangerous.

"You know where to find me if you need me," Stella said when she got up to quit.

"Sure," I said. "I'll phone in if there's anything out of the way in the Greenbach assignment."

"I'll be home all evening," Stella said. The brilliance of her smile lingered in the office a long time after she'd left it. I sat and listened to the noise of the creaking elevator going down. Then I was alone with the smog and traffic noises and my own heavy thoughts.

3

The house I wanted was a low, unpretentious Spanish-style property with a green-tiled roof and a barbecue patio set back behind well-shaved lawns about half a mile up Laurel Canyon. I arrived there a little short of six and went on past. Then I came back and parked about a hundred yards down, on the opposite side of the road, facing into L.A.

Looked like Greenbach was still home. Leastways, there were lights on in the house and a maroon station-wagon parked in front of the porch. I set fire to a cigarette and waited. That was something I was used to in my business.

Twenty minutes passed. Dusk had fallen with the suddenness it always has in these parts. There was a cool breeze and the scent of tropical flowers coming with it. It was one of the best times of the day and I was enjoying it to the full. I finished the cigarette and started another. While I was doing that the lights in the main rooms of the bungalow went out and the porch-light winked on. A few more minutes crawled by.

A lot of nothing was happening. That too was a constant factor in my business. You're bleeding all over the sidewalk, Mike, I told myself; how else could you earn a thousand bucks for sitting in the driving seat of your auto on such a great evening? I almost kidded myself. I was forgetting the other evenings when I finished up among the trash-cans, worked over. It evens out, Mike, I told myself. It evens out.

I crushed out my second butt in the dash-tray. I was becoming a regular Emily Dickinson at the age of thirty-three.

I looked in the rear mirror. Nothing moved in all the long expanse of road under the bloom of the street lamps atop their steel poles. I sighed. Seemed like it might be a long one. That was when the porch-light went out. I waited. The heavy tread of a man's footsteps sounded on the cement path.

I saw the dim shadow in the light from the street. The man got into the maroon station-wagon, the door slamming heavily. As he pulled down the driveway on to the highway I already had my motor started. I pulled quietly out, letting him get a couple of hundred yards away. Another car came out of a side-entrance a little way down, getting between me and Greenbach's vehicle. I put on my main beam then and settled down to follow.

We drove about ten miles before Greenbach pulled off the main-stem into a parking lot where green neon spelled out GARIBALDI in the velvet darkness. I signalled and pulled over, slotting the Buick in at the far end of the lot. I killed the motor and sat listening to the shirring of whitewall tyres going by on the freeway beyond.

Greenbach didn't seem to be in any hurry. I waited five minutes before he got out and went up the broad steps underneath the neon sign. I locked the

Buick and followed at my leisure, my nostrils catching again the perfume of tropical plants set in trunking at the side of the parking-lot and the stench of high-octane from the highway beyond.

Garibaldi's was and is a high-class roadhouse which does a little gambling on the side in private rooms on the third floor. Greenbach was at the top of the steps now. A thin stream of people were going in and out the big plate-glass doors. I went on in over a cool, tiled patio where fountains played in green copper basins and golden carp swam, half-visible between the fronds of tropical plants. It smelt fresh and good after the heat of the highway and I could feel my shirt sticking to my back.

Greenbach had disappeared into a washroom so I hung around near the reception area, looking at a giant fresco of Garibaldi and the Thousand wading ashore in Sicily or wherever it was they were supposed to have liberated. I looked for the Thousand but there were only about a dozen people in the painting. I frowned. Maybe history had lied. Or the artist had run out of materials. Either way it made a good subject for the lobby of a Californian road-house. I grinned. You're getting cynical, Mike, I told myself. I allow myself that observation two or three times on every case.

Greenbach was out the washroom now, making for the restaurant area. I kept on looking at the fresco but instead watching the doctor's reflection in the plate-glass window of a boutique set next to it. Greenbach hesitated and then went up another flight of steps into The Palermo Room. I waited at a table for two on the far side of the room, near the window.

The Captain of Waiters, a character with more gold braid than Admiral Nimitz and a sneering smile that revealed two gold teeth was at my elbow now. Fortunately, I hadn't yet eaten so I was genuinely hungry. Even so, this character was enough to put one off the food. He wheeled up to me like he was on a skateboard and put his fingers under my elbow.

"This way, sir," he said steering me in the opposite direction I wanted to go.

I shook my head.

"I want near the window."

He opened up the golden smile another three millimetres.

"All booked up, sir."

"I'll bet," I said.

I glanced around the room.

"You're expecting a big rush, I suppose?"

Gold-teeth looked pained.

"The window-seats always get booked, sir."

"Like hell they do," I said. "You'd better unbook one. That one there will do me nicely."

The Captain of Waiters smiled uneasily.

"I'll see what we can do, sir."

He took the five-spot I'd stuffed into the top pocket of his jacket. It disappeared so fast it just seemed to melt in his palm.

"Certainly, sir. I think we just got a cancellation."

"I thought you might have," I said.

★ ★ ★

He led the way across and seated me at the next table but one to Greenbach.

I was about fifteen feet away but as Greenbach was sideways on to me it didn't matter. The admiral had signalled another waiter over and I ordered a highball while I studied the menu, which was printed on a piece of timber about four feet long and two wide. It tired my arm after a bit so I lowered it against the table centre-piece and watched Greenbach over the top of it.

He was a short, stocky man, going bald on the crown of the head. He had black hair at the temple, rather long and ragged, which gave him the look of a somewhat rakish monk. He was about forty-five, I should have said, but looked a good deal older.

He had a plump, fleshy face with a dark complexion beneath the California tan. He was so swarthy he looked like a picture sent badly by wire, there was so much stubble on his chin and jowls. His eyebrows were black and heavily tufted and perspiration glistened among the folds of his face.

The mouth was firm and sensitive, the nose strong and slightly hooked. When he opened his mouth to give an order to the waiter his face was quite transformed. He had the most perfect set of teeth I'd ever seen on a male. Either that or he had the best dental crowning expert in the L.A. basin. The effect was so dazzling it was like sunshine flooding into the restaurant.

It made a remarkable transformation in the waiter too; he was almost singing as he ambled away to fill the doc's order. I turned back to the menu but kept tabs on Greenbach from time to time. He wore a lightweight grey suit that was impeccably tailored but the effect was spoiled by the sweat-stains in the small of the back. What made it worse was that there were old stains overlaid by the new ones.

He wore a cream silk shirt that looked like he hadn't worn it more than five or six days and a pale blue polka-dot bow tie that floated like a huge butterfly under his double-chin. I sat and admired the effect for a while. It was all I had to do until my order came and they certainly took their time here.

I got my drink in the end and sat back and sipped it carefully, making it last. Then I remembered that Dillon was picking up the tab. I finished it and ordered another. By this time the place was filling up a little and the brittle fragments of conversation started reverberating against the high, white-painted ceiling.

I had been sitting there about half an hour, looking casually about me, the chit-chat washing over me, when I picked up a tall, blonde girl who was slowly swimming into focus. She passed my table and went on over to where Greenbach was sitting. He got up as she arrived and waved her into a chair. I studied her as she sat down. She was facing toward me and it wasn't a difficult thing to do.

She was about twenty-five, five feet ten inches tall, and had a slim, willowy body, nicely tanned. I could see a lot of it because she had on a white top which left her mid-riff and arms and shoulders bare. The white tailored slacks cut across just above where her navel would have been and were secured with a big, brass-buckled leather belt.

She had a wispy pink scarf which seemed to float against the brownness of her throat and she looked altogether too friendly and clinging toward a man of Greenbach's looks and years. I grinned and took my first sip of my second drink. You're getting sour in your old age, Mike, I told myself.

The waiter was back again now, with the thoughtful look in his eye that waiters get when you aren't justifying the joint's overheads. The girl and the doctor were ordering things from the menu with reckless extravagance so I went over the moon as well. I sent for a steak and a salad with ice-cream and coffee to follow. Then I settled back and studied my nails while keeping tabs on the couple over by the window.

The girl looked almost Scandinavian. She had tawny blonde hair that hung in long swathes down to her shoulders. Her brow was broad and her eyebrows looked natural, not plucked. She wore a minimum of makeup and her face glowed with health and vitality. She had a straight nose; very blue eyes; broad, white teeth and full pink lips that opened frequently to smile. I could have sat and watched her for years without tiring.

My meal arrived then and provided a diversion. Throughout it I kept an eye on Greenbach and the girl. They were chatting animatedly. Normally I'm pretty good at lip-reading but I couldn't get much this evening. An occasional "darling" from the girl; the knife and fork work was interfering with the dialogue. I gave it up in the end and concentrated on my own food.

As I ate I kept tabs on the tables in the rest of the room. Leastways, those in the section of the restaurant nearest. I couldn't see anything suspicious. I figured someone else might have been tailing Greenbach. That would make sense and was possibly the reason Dillon had hired me. But there was no-one in the room that I could see who had the slightest interest in the couple over by the window. And I've been at the business quite a few years now.

I finished the meal and ordered a large coffee. I sat and drank it and stared through my cigarette smoke. The blonde number had had several drinks before the meal; wine with it; and two or three liqueurs after. She was obviously feeling the effects by now and her laughter was a little too frequent and a little too loud. It was beginning to attract attention from the surrounding tables and I could see Greenbach gaze anxiously at the girl from time to time.

They got up to go after another ten minutes. I called for my check, paid it and was out near the restaurant entrance by the time they had gotten down the stairs. Greenbach was standing in the foyer studying a poster. The girl had gone to the cloakroom I figured. I didn't hang around but went out to the parking-lot. I sat behind the wheel of the Buick and smoked.

I looked at my watch. It was just coming up to nine o'clock. I glanced at the dark, sardonic reflection of my face in the windshield. For once it didn't seem a bad way to make a living. The rain had stopped some hours previously and it was now a fine, dry night.

I sat there for another quarter hour. Then Greenbach and the blonde number came down the steps of Garibaldi's. He had to half support her and he looked anxiously about him in the dusk of the parking-lot. There was some argument between them. Apparently they couldn't make up their mind which car to take. Then Greenbach led the way over to the maroon station-wagon. He opened the door and the blonde slid into the passenger seat.

Greenbach went round and got heavily behind the wheel. I waited until he'd started his motor and eased up toward the entrance of the parking-lot. Then I started mine. He'd turned right. I could see his rear-lights snaking up a secondary road into the hills. I gave him a discreet start and pulled out to follow.

4

We drove for about another dozen miles, going uphill all the time. I stayed well back, keeping tabs by the headlight reflections in the sky ahead. I had switched off my main beams and was driving on sidelights only, which made things difficult. Trees and brush grew close to the road here, which cast the edge in deep shadow and I had some anxious moments as the Buick skittered round the bends.

The road zigzagged for about five miles but then straightened out a little. I'd lost Greenbach's car temporarily and eased back to about twenty m.p.h just in case he'd stopped around a bend. There was nothing else on the road at all, which was unusual, and I didn't want to run on to him without warning.

I needn't have worried; he'd gone straight on and didn't seem to be keeping any watch in his rear-mirror or he must have spotted my side-lights at some period. Presently I came to a high bluff along which the road ran in long, shallow curves, and I picked up the headlights again, about half a mile ahead and way out to my left.

It was bright moonlight so I doused my sidelights for a couple of minutes, while I was running along the exposed edge of the road facing him across a deep valley. The view was pretty spectacular and any other time I would have enjoyed it. But not tonight. Not under these circumstances and on a tail job I didn't know anything about. I wondered what Dillon's motive was. He'd impressed me as a smart cookie and I figured he wouldn't have sent me out unless there'd been some real danger to his client.

I was back in the shade of trees now, still running along the bluff, so I flicked on my sidelights, frowning ahead to where the moonlight made a stippled pattern of silver through the tunnel of boughs on the smooth surface of the road. I looked at my fuel gauge. I had plenty of gas, but it pays to make sure. I'd been caught once before through concentrating on the job and forgetting the fuel level. That night I'd had a fifteen-mile walk to a gas station and a blown case for my trouble.

I couldn't see Greenbach's vehicle now but I didn't think there was anywhere along here he could turn off without me seeing him; I opened the dash cubby and got out my large-scale. I studied it in the available light coming in through the windshield. It was out of the trees now and it was pretty bright; I found the road after a few seconds but the shadows on the paper made it impossible to make out the detail. I gave it up after a bit and concentrated on the driving.

A couple of cars passed me, going in the opposite direction; that was an event up here tonight. The road was fairly straight now and I picked up Greenbach's rear-lights going round the next bend. I hoped it wouldn't be too long a drive. Maybe Greenbach intended to stay the night at a motel somewhere. Seemed highly likely judging by the company he was keeping.

I grinned. Somehow I couldn't see myself crouching outside a motel window taking notes for Dillon. The money was good, sure, but that wasn't my style. The Smith-Wesson made a heavy pressure against my shoulder muscles as I tooled the Buick round the next bend. Greenbach's car was out of sight again but I could make out the headlights above the trees. A few houses were coming up and what seemed to be a small settlement.

I throttled back. We were up to a cross-roads now and the shimmer of neon from a small road-house showed. Greenbach turned right and I let him get well away before making the turn. He was already a quarter of a mile up the highway before I hit the straight. The houses were thinning out and long before I got to it Greenbach took a side-lane which led off uphill to the left. Looked like it might be the end of the trip.

I idled up to the lane entrance. The headlights were cutting wide swathes through the night ahead. I switched off my sidelights and drove on into the dusty side-road. There was just about

41

room for two vehicles to pass but I hoped I wouldn't be meeting anyone else this evening. I kept a careful eye on the progress of Greenbach's heap. It was quiet up here and I'd have to stop before he did. Otherwise he'd hear my engine coming up the lane in such a quiet spot.

It was a delicate balance. I looked out for a place where the lane might widen. If it wasn't too far I might park there and walk on ahead. There had to be a house. Greenbach wouldn't just come up here to park in a field. Sure, he could do his necking like that but he wouldn't come all this way. There were plenty places more convenient for that purpose. I grinned. Boyhood memories coming back, Faraday, I told myself.

I eased off and the Buick rumbled to a walking pace. The moonlight was brilliant on the dusty road ahead and a grove of trees at the roadside stood out starkly, like an etching. At the same miment I saw the main beams of Greenbach's vehicle flicker over the façade of a big, white-painted building about a quarter of a mile ahead. I pulled right across the lane, drew the Buick on to the grass verge beneath the trees and killed the motor.

Apart from the shrilling of cicadas there was nothing but the faint sigh of the breeze in the tree-tops. I eased out the driving seat and stretched myself, quietly closing the door behind me. I checked on the Smith-Wesson shells, replaced the safety and put the weapon back in the nylon holster. I could still hear the noise of Greenbach's automobile motor from across the fields.

Then it stopped and the light of the main beams went out. I sighed. I got to the side of the road. Dust rose heavily as I started padding up toward the house.

★ ★ ★

The place was farther than I thought. It was nearer three quarters of a mile and I was sweating when I got there. There were lights on in the porch and in the house itself. It was a big, Spanish-style mansion, painted white with a green-tiled roof. I could see that because there was a heartshaped swimpool up on the terrace and the floodlighting was on there.

There were white picket fences at the entrance; a big, horse-shoe shaped area of turf with a pink-floored driveway making the U of the horse-shoe and containing the lawn between it. In front of the house there was a crescent-shaped concourse; the right-hand side led to the terrace and the swimpool. The left to a four-car garage and what looked like a stable block. I stood in the moonlight, keeping behind a clump of jacarandas whose perfume was cloying this time of night and frowned at the spread. Stella hadn't been exaggerating.

If this belonged to Greenbach as well he must be very wealthy indeed. The Laurel Canyon house would have cost me five years' salary and according to Stella, Greenbach owned at least three properties like this. It's an uneven world, Faraday, I told myself. I grinned. You've always known that, Mike, I added. I got over the low picket fence and eased on to the emerald turf to the shadow cast by flowering shrubs.

I kept well away from the swimpool area and its floodlighting and concentrated on the turf and the dark places. I wasn't doing so badly either. In three minutes I'd halved the distance between me and the house and I still had plenty of shadow. Problem was how to get around in rear where I sensed the action might be. Though what I hoped to find out I wasn't sure. But I intended to earn Dillon's money. He must have had a good reason asking me to keep tabs and I always tried to give value for my fee.

I glanced back at the road. Nothing moved in the moonlight, though I could see headlamp beams flickering along the faint ribbon some miles off. I shrugged. If anyone came along I'd hear. Sure, I could easily be seen against the whiteness of the house. But someone would have to come along the lane on foot to see me. I figured there wasn't much chance of that.

I was up near the edge of the lawn now, in deep shadow. I had become aware a little earlier of faint music from the house and now it was stronger, a heavy beat resounding below a vibrato jazz trumpet. I figured Greenbach and his girl-friend had a hi-fi going. I worked my way toward the façade of the building, still in shadow and then risked it across a short stretch of open grass, masked from the house at this point by a white trellised archway.

There were French doors, uncurtained, a little farther along but they were in the glare thrown by the swimpool floodlights so I didn't figure there would be any point in going there. Not unless I wanted to advertise my presence. I was looking for darkness and concealing shrubbery and I wouldn't find it on this side of the house. So I turned left and kept going, not hanging around the porch area, but making for the stable block now that I was again hidden from the main house by foliage.

The windows in this section of the house were dark. I got halfway between the main drive and the concourse when the porch lights went out. The going was easier now. I spent a while crossing the pink tarmac and presently found a big iron gate that evidently led to the rear of the grounds.

I eased through it without too much noise and found myself in another paved area. The wind was gusting a little now and the noise it made in the tree-tops would have masked my movements in any case. I got back on to grass and headed away from the stabling back toward the main house. There were flowering hedges and a square, sunken pool and then I was out on to open terrace. Lights were spilling from big picture windows on to the terrazzo tiling and I padded on down, keeping below the level of the darkened windows I passed.

As I got closer I could hear the hi-fi again. The main windows of the room I wanted were closed but I could see the big louvres at the top were open. I covered about half the distance between the edge of the terrace when the lights were lowered. A faint illumination now came from the picture windows like there were only a couple of desk lamps on. That suited me fine and I was able to make better progress.

I got about five yards from the windows when the hi-fi cut off. It was so quick it almost caught me out. The scratching made by my size nines on the edge of the tiled path bordering the lawn sounded like it could have been heard back in L.A. I went to ground in some shrubbery under the window and waited. I could feel my heart thumping like a steamboat engine and sweat trickled down my collar.

Nothing happened and I got up in the end. Your reflexes are great but your nerves are all shot to hell, Faraday, I told myself. I grinned crookedly and waited another couple of minutes. I could hear faint voices now. I eased back toward the windows. There was a strange flickering coming from the room, like the people in it had a TV set on.

I had to be careful over the last few yards. There was still quite a lot of illumination in the room, despite the lowering of the lighting. Some of it spilled out on to the terrace and I didn't aim to find myself centre-stage with an audience of two inside. Somehow I knew it would be just the two. If this was Greenbach's house the set-up at the restaurant and the long drive out here led to only one conclusion.

In other words I didn't expect them to be watching TV or listening to hi-fi. Leastways, only that, I corrected myself. And this might be one of the spin-offs of the unproductive sort of tail-job Dillon had landed me with.

I was up at the window now. I got underneath the ledge at the far edge and cautiously raised my eyes to sill level. It took me a little while before my eyes became adjusted. It was quite a surprise and not at all what I'd expected.

5

I blinked. The blonde number sat at a desk inside the big room, which was decked out as a library. She was certainly a lot more sober than she appeared in the restaurant. Dr Greenbach sat a couple of yards off from her. Contrary to expectation they weren't even looking at one another. Their eyes were fixed in front of them.

Greenbach had a small electronic device on the desk before him like the remote switch for a TV set. I looked more closely, noted the thick black flex which snaked from it, went down the side of the desk and disappeared across the carpet. I sighed. It was a remote control switch for a TV set.

The set itself was a big console job at the far side of the room. It was set at an angle so I couldn't see the screen. And in any event it was blocked off from me because of the open wing of the right-hand door which normally closed off the screen when the set wasn't in use. But it was definitely on because there was a blueish-white flickering light coming from it. The strobing effect made strange striped masks of the faces of the doctor and the girl.

The doctor pressed the switch and changed the channel. I knew that because the pattern on their faces altered abruptly. I half-knelt below the window for what must have been fifteen minutes but seemed like a couple of years. During that time all Greenbach did was to change channels. He must have switched to a dozen or more in the time I was there.

The girl sat and watched without saying anything, though she seemed to be scribbling in a notebook. They were the most restless TV watchers I'd ever seen in my life. Unless they were looking for a particular programme and couldn't come up with it. I tried shifting around but I still couldn't see the screen. Basically, the set was facing away from the window and it was quite impossible.

I made a note of the time. I'd check

on tonight's programmes when I got back into L.A. and see if there might be a lead there. There was something definitely crazy about the whole set-up. Firstly, Greenbach didn't strike me as the sort of character who'd be interested in television anyway. And I'd expected him to bring the girl out here for something else entirely.

Thirdly, no one in their senses would watch TV in this manner. Fourthly, and this was perhaps the most important factor, both Greenbach and the blonde number were watching the screen as though their lives depended on it. I eased my cramped limbs and dropped down below the level of the window ledge.

The moon was still bright and the heavy, cloying perfume of tropical vegetation was drifting over from the garden. It was so heavy it almost made my senses swim. Either that or I was a little dizzy from being in such a cramped position for so long. When I eased up to the window level again the programme viewing seemed to have settled down. The couple in the room were still intent on the screen but the light from it was even and steady on their faces.

I put my ear up close to the glass, as high as I dared, but I couldn't hear the sound. It might have given me an idea of the programme. Then I saw that the window was fitted with double glazing; it was tightly shut, despite the heat of the night. That was crazy too; even with air-conditioning most normal people prefer to have their windows open on such nights. I gave up. I caught the heavy perfume of flowers again as I got down on the terrace. My eyes felt heavy and tired.

The wind was gusting a little now and I was startled to hear something that sounded like a door slamming in the distance. I glanced around. Nothing moved in the night except the shadows of foliage on the paving of the terrace and the restless fret of the branches themselves. I moved a little way down the façade of the house but I couldn't see anything. Maybe it had been just an insecure door in the garage area.

When I got back to the window the action had changed. Greenbach and the girl had given up their TV watching. The girl sat smoking at the side of the table, watching the doctor. He was unplugging the TV controls from the machine. As I got up to the glass he coiled the cable and rolled it up round the switch. He put the whole thing in a small black briefcase he took from the table at his side.

My eyelids felt heavy again. I rubbed them and eased back from the window. My eyes were watering, my vision blurred. I tried to focus up on the wall in front of me. It looked vague and insubstantial. I tried to get up, found I couldn't make it. Perspiration was cascading down my face. The outlines of Greenbach's house started to waver. My legs felt like they were made of toothpaste. I went down and out so quickly I knew nothing about it.

★ ★ ★

When I came around it was still dark. A splintered shard of yellow resolved itself into the light spilling from the window of the room I'd been watching. The scene wavered for a minute or two and then focused up. I felt sick and could feel perspiration running down my face and onto my collar.

I was lying on my back, my head against the flagstones and a cool breeze blowing from the garden beyond had brought me around pretty quickly. Otherwise I wouldn't have made it. I made a slight movement with my right hand, reaching for the Smith-Wesson; couldn't find it. Slight as the movement had been it attracted someone's attention.

A dark figure was crouching in front of the window, occupying the position I'd taken up. He was looking intently into the room so I couldn't make out the face. He was small and wiry and appeared to be dressed in dark trousers and a black sweater. He turned around toward me. I froze, closing my eyes again. The silence continued. When I opened my lids again the dark man was still looking into the room.

My head was clear now. I started to

get up. About the same time I spotted the Smith-Wesson. It was lying just off the terrace, in the small runnel between the rough stones and the grass. The dark figure abruptly rose. I slumped back on the terrace, watching from between half-closed lids. The face turned toward me was a crumpled ruin, two dark holes for eyes; the nose bulbous and elongated, the mouth pulled down in a permanent rictus.

The figure came over to my side with incredible rapidity. It knelt, the face frozen and unreal. The rubber mask had been overdone but I couldn't prevent a reflex action in my belly muscles. The light from the window cast a glinting reflection as the switch-blade opened. I didn't wait for anything else; I was clear-headed and angry. The edge of my right hand came up and flailed cross the lower edge of the ruined face, connected hard with flesh and bone.

I had my knee in the belly before the cry of pain came out the mouth-slit. The knife struck sparks from the terrace stones as it fell and then I was rolling over, reaching for the Smith-Wesson. The dark figure somersaulted down the terrace. Then it was up again with snake-like speed. I kicked the flick-knife away and it fell somewhere outside the arc of light cast by the window.

My right foot struck the knife-artist in the shin and he skidded aside with a muffled grunt; he was pretty durable though. I'd gone over too far and missed the Smith-Wesson. I chopped the dark figure with the flat of my hand again but this time met solid shoulder muscle. He turned, steel-like fingers searching for my nostrils and eye-sockets. I felt blood run down my cheek; his finger-nails were as sharp as razor blades.

He was in hard condition and handled himself like a karate expert; he might have been Japanese or Korean from his build but it was hard to tell with the weird get-up. He was certainly stoical for any normal person would have howled with the punishment I'd already dished out. I didn't let it trouble my conscience; I'd have had my throat slit if I hadn't come around in time.

I side-stepped and caught him a karate chop to the neck muscles. I'd done a little judo in my time and this one went home; I heard him cough and fight for breath as I went back down the terrace for the gun.

I was just stooping for it when the room light went out. In the darkness the knife-artist misjudged and his shoulder struck the ground behind my legs, instead of hitting clean. I went spinning out over the lawn even so; it felt like I'd been shot through the calf. I figured his head must have hit a nerve in my leg. It paralysed me momentarily and I landed awkwardly on hard-baked turf, winding myself.

I hoped Greenbach and the girl hadn't heard the scuffle; maybe that was why they had turned out the light. A moment later I heard an automobile start up in front of the house. Guess they'd finished their TV programme or whatever it was and left. I heard the heavy tread of feet over the grass as the car gunned up. I was lying flat and could make out the figure in the faint light from the sky.

I hoped he hadn't found the Smith-Wesson. I wouldn't have much chance with my leg in the state it was in. He hadn't seen me, went too far out. I kicked his knee-caps with my good leg, giving it everything I had. He howled this time all right, cart-wheeling in pain. While he was doing that I dragged myself over to the terrace. I got to the Smith-Wesson this time, threw off the safety. The doc's car was well away now.

I could see its yellow headlights going away down the road. I loosed off a shot as my man got up. He took the hint. I caught a glimpse of him in the flash. He was making pretty good speed, despite his injuries. I grinned. I sat on the terrace and listened to him crashing through the under-growth. Presently another motor gunned. This time the lights went the other way. I got up. The evening's entertainment was over.

I went back up on the terrace. I risked the pencil-flash, found what I was looking for. Just a few fragments of very thin glass. The remains of the capsule containing the gas that had knocked me out. I went around the terrace but I couldn't find the pistol; they usually work by compressed air and are much favoured in espionage, especially by K.G.B. agents.

The flick-knife artist had been too curious. He should have cut my throat first, instead of going to look through the window. Though I was naturally glad he'd adopted that procedure. That meant two parties were now interested in Greenbach's doings. I decided to give things a miss for the rest of the evening. The doctor was probably going back to his house in L.A. anyway.

And anything else after this was bound to be anti-climax. But I had a lot to keep me occupied as I drove back to town.

6

"So what do we know?" Stella said.

I studied the long cut on my face in the telephone mirror. I slid it shut and put my feet up on my old broad-top.

"Nothing plus nothing is nothing," I said.

Stella smiled.

"About par for the course," she said.

I set fire to a cigarette and flipped the spent match stalk over in the direction of the earthenware tray on my desk. It bounced on the lip and skidded into the middle. Stella got up from her own desk and put it back in the tray with a sigh. She stood looking down at me silently for a moment. This morning she wore brown tailored slacks and a red silk shirt. The items seemed to have been painted on her flesh; the vibrations hurt my eyes every time she moved.

Stella smiled a secret smile again, like she knew what I was thinking. She went

61

over toward the glassed-in alcove where we do the brewing-up. I waited for the snick of the percolator going on. It wasn't raining today. It was only just eleven but already the heat was coming up from the sidewalk below like the kitchen of a Chinese hashhouse during the rush-hour. Stella put her head round the edge of the screen.

"I didn't ask," she said.

I grinned.

"You didn't have to," I told her.

Stella came back and sat on the edge of her desk, thoughtfully swinging one of her long legs. It was the right. That's a particularly good one. I stood it for a moment or two and then focused my eyes on the cracks in the ceiling.

"Let's see what we got," Stella said.

"After the coffee," I said. "I can face it better then."

Stella got up and went around the desk. She riffled in a bundle of paper stacked neatly at a corner of her blotter.

"Dillon rang in earlier," she said. "He wondered how you made out last night."

I feathered blue smoke at the ceiling, frowned at her.

"We agreed on a weekly report," I said. "He must want his pound of flesh."

Stella shrugged.

"He is paying top-dollar, Mike. And he probably feels he has the right to keep tabs."

"Sure," I said. "I'll maybe drop over later and give him an interim rundown."

Stella looked at me enigmatically.

"Della Strongman must have a personality as evocative as her name," she said.

I grinned.

"Nothing like that, honey."

Stella went back to the alcove without replying. I heard the clinking of cups and caught the aroma of freshly roasted beans. She came back and put the cup down on my blotter, pushed the biscuit tin toward me. I took down my feet from the desk-top and eased back in my swivel chair.

Stella was back at her own desk now. She looked at me with very blue eyes over the rim of her cup.

"So Greenbach's fond of television?" she said at last.

"Seems like it," I said.

Stella frowned.

"What about the blonde girl, Mike? Shouldn't be too difficult to trace."

"Assuming I wanted to trace her," I said. "My brief was to look out for Greenbach."

"You did that all right," Stella said. "Being jumped. You and Greenbach both could have been killed."

I shook my head, watching my smoke rings eddying up to the ceiling and being caught in the draught from the plastic fan.

"Only me," I said.

Stella looked at me.

"How do you figure that?"

"The guy in the mask wasn't there to kill Greenbach," I said. "He had plenty of time to do that through the window while I was out. He was keeping tabs on him."

Stella put down her coffee cup with a faint chink above the distant traffic noises.

"But why would he want to kill you, Mike?"

"I was in his way," I said. "He was obviously already in the garden. Maybe he intended to use the gas pistol on Greenbach and kidnap him. Dillon might know why. But there were too many snags. Myself and the girl. I figure the Hallowe'en character hoped to find Greenbach alone. He obviously knows the properties he owns and his movements."

Stella brushed an imaginary strand of blonde hair back from her immaculate coiffure.

"Because he was already there?"

I nodded.

"The only way to read it. He didn't follow us out from L.A. or I'd have seen him. Therefore he knew the address and that the doc was going to be there."

Stella picked up her coffee cup again.

"Looks like a puzzle, Mike."

"Which is where I came in," I said.

Stella got up and brought me a refill.

"You going to level with Dillon, Mike?"

I shook my head.

"He hasn't exactly been expansive with me. I'll tell him about the girl and the visit to the house. I'll leave out the bit about me being put out."

I shifted in my chair.

"I don't want to spoil my image."

"That'll be the day," Stella said. "Shouldn't you be keeping tabs on Greenbach?"

"He's at his laboratory until five," I said. "I'll pick him up later."

She stood and looked down at me mockingly.

"What are you doing for lunch?"

"I'll get outside a beer and a sandwich somewhere," I said.

Stella made a moue.

"I'm in funds today, Mike. I was going to stand treat."

"In that case, be my guest," I said.

★ ★ ★

Dillon leaned back in his chair and nodded moodily. It was raining again now and driblets of moisture were running down the windows of his office in the Schuyler Building and blurring the landscape outside. It looked like the whole of the L.A. basin was weeping. It didn't seem to do much about the heat though. It might have been steam for all the good the rain was doing in that direction.

Today Dillon had forsaken the yachting blazer and wore a light-weight grey suit, impeccably styled. It was supposed to make him look like a clean-cut young executive. He was around fifteen years too old for that but he still looked pretty good. He gave his strong white teeth an airing and fiddled with a pen-set on the blotter in front of him.

"It doesn't seem much for what we're paying, Mr Faraday," he said haughtily through his teeth.

"What did you expect? The St Valentine's Day massacre?" I said.

I leaned over and deposited an inch of ash from my cigarette into his desk tray.

"You hired me to look out for Greenbach. Not to fall down on the job. No news is good news in your book, surely."

Dillon started as though he'd been stung by a horse-fly. His chintzy features looked a little frayed at the edges. A pink flush started round his nostrils, went clear out to his ear-lobes. It couldn't go any farther without utilizing Disney techniques, so it started coming back in again. He cleared his throat with a low rasping noise.

"It isn't your function, Faraday . . . " he began.

"And it isn't my function taking a case without knowing what the hell I'm at," I interrupted.

Dillon's façade cracked right up. He looked pained. Then he forced a reluctant smile. He lifted up one well-manicured hand from the blotter and looked at it reverently, as though he had diamond-tipped finger nails.

"Don't let's get sore, Faraday," he said.

He smiled again, lifting his deep tan and expensive hair-cut up from the blotter to face me.

"There is something in what you say."

"Who's sore?" I said, "I'm just stating facts. Just because there's nothing startling to report doesn't mean I'm falling down on the job."

"No one was suggesting it," he said, somewhat less stiffly.

The air was clearing. He fooled around with the penset some more, pulling his fleshy mouth about as though he had inner troubles.

"Do you mind giving it me again. It seems such a pointless way of spending the evening."

"It was what I thought at the time," I said. "Especially as I was outside on the terrace."

"Quite," he said hastily. "But perhaps there's something you overlooked."

I shook my head.

"I'm not in the habit of overlooking things, Mr Dillon. But I'll re-cap if it'll make you any happier. Like I said, I picked up Greenbach at his Laurel Canyon place and tailed him to Garibaldi's. It's a roadhouse."

"I know it," Dillon said. "He's used it

a number of times before."

"He was joined for dinner by the blonde number," I said. "I've already described her. You haven't yet said whether you know her or not."

"I may do," Dillon said evasively.

He looked distinctly unhappy sitting there behind the desk. He didn't impress me very much on this occasion. The same thought may have crossed his own mind because he was examining his nails again.

"The girl got really sauced up," I said. "I naturally expected the evening to be far different from the way it turned out."

Dillon smiled faintly.

"Naturally," he said.

I rode along with that one.

"Like I said I followed them when they left the place. They went up into the hills to another property Greenbach owns. It's at . . ."

"I know," Dillon interrupted. "My secretary's got a note of all his addresses."

"We're in rich company," I said. "To make a short story shorter they went inside and I crept around in rear. They were in a room overlooking the terrace, watching TV. Greenbach sat at the table and the girl opposite. I stayed there quite a while. They weren't necking or drinking. They just sat watching TV."

Dillon looked at me moodily. His eyes were searching my face like he expected to catch me out in a lie. I was too old a hand for that. Dillon was used to court-room procedures. I'd weighed him up as a pretty shrewd apple.

He was too good at detecting hesitation or evasion on people's faces. He'd had too much practice at it. So I didn't tell him any lies. I just left things out. That made it much simpler. You got real ethics, Faraday, I told myself. Dillon grunted and sat upright in his chair like he'd been on the point of falling asleep. Maybe he had at that.

"And that was it?"

I nodded.

"I stayed there a while longer but absolutely nothing happened. They just switched off the TV and then came away."

Dillon sighed regretfully.

71

"You didn't see what programme?"

I looked at him blankly. He went faintly pink around the gills.

"I just wondered."

"Sure," I said. "The screen was away from me. It didn't seem particularly important at the time."

Dillon nodded again and half closed his eyes.

"Maybe you could give Miss Strongman a rundown on the evening on your way out. I'd like to get it on record."

"If it's important."

Dillon looked at me levelly.

"Everything's important in my business, Mr Faraday. And as long as I'm calling the shots I'd like Miss Strongman's note."

I shrugged and got up.

"Why not?" I said. "You're saving me typing paper."

Dillon looked at me steadily.

"What's that cut on your face?"

"I was standing too close to the razor."

Dillon smiled faintly. I stopped at the door but he didn't say anything, just went on sitting there fooling with his pen-set. I opened the door and went on out.

7

The girl at the desk lazily uncoiled herself from the swivel chair and looked at me with haughty eyes as I came out Dillon's office. Della Strongman still wore the cream linen suit and the scarlet silk scarf round her neck, though some of the starch had disappeared from her manner. She patted a leather chair at the side of her desk and I sat down.

"Dillon tells me you have a report to make," she said.

"Mr Dillon," I said.

She grinned suddenly. She looked astonishingly beautiful as she did so. It was the first genuine and human reaction I'd noticed about her.

"He doesn't pay me well enough to rate a prefix," she said.

I stared at the little leather cylinder that held her scarf together. She passed a pink tongue over white teeth and looked at me mockingly with the steady grey eyes.

"I use it for a message pouch," she said. "On Dillon's special assignments."

"It looks better on you than boy scouts," I said.

I put my hand out and fingered the leather toggle. She stirred slightly in the chair and flushed. She put up a pink-nailed hand to pat her hair. The long eye-lashes flickered once or twice and she had recovered herself. She put cool fingers on mine, took my hand down from her throat.

"No window-shopping," she said.

I leaned back in my chair and took in all the equipment on view.

"What does that mean?"

She shrugged.

"Read it any way you like. About this stuff for Dillon . . . "

"It'll keep," I said. "What do you do after hours?"

The insolent look was back on her face again now.

"Curl up with a good book."

I grinned.

"I'll bet. Mind if I smoke?"

She said nothing but indicated the

metal ash-tray on the desk in front of her. I set fire to a cigarette and put the spent match-stalk in the tray. She watched me cautiously from beneath half-lowered eyelids, as though she expected me to make a pass at her. I wouldn't have minded except it was a public place and it was too hot anyway.

I gave her the report. She didn't say anything but covered the pages of her notebook with precise, impeccable shorthand as I went on. I looked over my shoulder presently and found Dillon standing in his doorway quietly watching us. I turned back to the girl and smiled to myself. I went on dictating and then I heard the soft snick as Dillon shut his door again.

"Velvet heels," Della Strongman went on.

She finished off her notes with a flourish and put down the book on the desk. She glanced at one flawless knee that was angled casually from beneath her short skirt.

"You know the Astor Bar?"

"Who doesn't" I said.

She looked at me critically, the tip of her tongue visible between the full, sensuous lips.

"Meet you there at eight o'clock tomorrow night. And don't be late."

"I got my Good Conduct Badge for punctuality," I said.

She smiled a secret smile. She was already turning back to her notes as I made the outer door.

I buttoned the elevator and waited, listening to the brittle pecking of electric typewriters from behind the closed doors of the offices. When the teak cage whined to a stop there were only two people in it. They both got off. The same elevator-boy was in charge. The character about sixty-five with the silvered hair like a toilet brush. He greeted me like I was a close relative he hadn't seen for thirty years. I've often noticed that with elevator-operators. It must be one of the most boring jobs of all time.

"See they got two more snipers on the freeway," he said. "It's getting to be a terrible world."

I gave him one of my sympathetic

looks. He stopped at the second floor before I could think of anything suitable to say. Not that it seemed to make any difference. These characters can make with the conversation even when they're on their own.

A girl got on at the second floor. I'd seen her before. She gave me a frank look. There was something carnal in the open appraisal of the eyes. Whatever it was I liked it.

"Great day, Miss Popkiss," the elevator-boy said with enthusiasm.

Her eyes glanced over him without seeing him.

"If you like water," she said.

Her eyes brushed back over me with an almost sensual caressing glance. I was sorry we were only two floors up. The ride could have lasted an hour for all I cared.

Miss Popkiss wore the same outfit as on the previous occasion. The blue linen shirt and the pale blue slacks looked like they'd been poured on. She carried a white raincoat over one bronzed arm and a small dark red leather shoulder-bag with a big strap that depended from her left shoulder. Her teeth glinted very white in her mouth as she glanced toward the door as the next set of people got on.

At the ground floor she walked off with an athletic ripple that set nerves flaming in me all the way down to my fallen arches. I followed her out, trying to concentrate but making a poor job of it. I was due to pick up Greenbach again soon. As a commission it was definitely humdrum but as Stella said the money was good. And I'd never been one to argue with money so long as it was properly earned.

I got out the lobby of the Schuyler Building and watched the dark number walk across to a scarlet sedan in the main parking lot. She got in and gunned off, driving westward across the city. I watched her exhaust smoke out of sight and then got my own heap. I was feeling more discontented than ever by the time I got to Greenbach's laboratory.

This was in a high wire-fence compound on the perimeter of Arnos Chemicals complex over in the industrial section of town. The smog, combined with the fall-out from the tall chimneys made a nice backdrop. There was a space outside the wire for public parking and I slotted the Buick in and sat incinerating a cigarette while I kept tabs on the low, white, temporary-looking buildings that housed the labs.

Greenbach looked to be a little late today. I checked on my watch. It was after five-fifteen and he usually showed around five. It was clouding up a little and trying to rain again but it was holding off for the moment. The heat was at its stickiest though. That was true to form. I'd have preferred the rain which would have cleared the atmosphere.

I sat and finished my cigarette and listened to a radio bulletin and watched the grit gathering on the windshield of the Buick and thought about my life and my prospects. That didn't take me long. In the background automobiles were back-firing and gunning up and every so often the blue-uniformed guard at the compound gate would wave through someone from the lab area.

I finished the cigarette, stubbed it out in the dash-board tray and set fire to another. An old Guy Lombardo record was coming over now. I flipped the switch and killed the syrup. You'll be drowning in waves of nostalgia next, Mike, I told myself.

Just then I saw Greenbach's heap coming through the gate. I switched on the motor and idled out to the edge of the parking strip. Greenbach turned the nose of his vehicle. I sighed. This was one hell of an assignment. I pulled out to follow.

★ ★ ★

The traffic was thickening up like usual and it wasn't difficult to let Greenbach's automobile get two or three cars ahead. He wasn't using the scarlet station-wagon today but a dark, anonymous-looking Studebaker so I couldn't afford to let him get too far ahead. I jotted down the licence-plate details just in case and pulled the magnetic scratch-pad higher up the instrument panel where I could read it off in a hurry. That made me feel a little happier.

He kept a pretty steady pace, around forty, but there was a break in his usual pattern. Before, he'd gone back to his Laurel Canyon house but this time he was heading downtown. It wasn't the week-end and there was no other discernible reason for the break in the pattern. He could have been having a meal at a restaurant before going home, it was true, but somehow I didn't think so. He'd pulled in in front of a drug-store before I'd fitted my thoughts together and I almost lost him.

I waited until the traffic-lights had changed to green, found another slot a little beyond and parked, keeping my eyes glued to the rear mirror. Greenbach went on over to a news-stand near the drug-store and bought an *Examiner*. Then he went on into the store. Maybe he was just buying a tube of aspirin. Or then again he might have been making a phone-call. It wasn't worth getting out to make sure. He could have been away before I made it back to the Buick.

Then again he might merely have run out of toilet-rolls. I exposed my teeth to myself in the rear-mirror. It's the only relaxation I get on this sort of case and I rate it pretty highly. Greenbach was away about fifteen minutes. It was then I found I was parked in front of a fire-plug. Another car in front pulled out and I moved down before any passing cop noticed. By this time Greenbach was crossing the sidewalk to his own heap so I kept the motor running.

I looked in the mirror. Greenbach sat behind the wheel studying the newspaper. He sat there for about ten minutes. I switched off the motor. That was when he started up the Studebaker, pulling out into the traffic. I sighed. Jesus, Mike, I told myself, it's days like this that one questions the whole system.

Fortunately, there was a lot of stuff passing so I had time to start up myself and edge out. Greenbach drove a mile or two toward town and then made a U-turn in a section where this was allowed. By the time I'd made the same manoeuvre

I'd lost him. He'd turned off to the left, between the walls of two big warehouses in an industrial section and when I made the turn, tyres squealing in the heat, the road ahead was blank.

I drove on cautiously, dropping back to twenty miles an hour, looking at the intersections. Fortunately there wasn't anywhere much he could have turned off; there was a big hump in the road about half a mile ahead and when I breasted it I could see the black Studebaker cruising on slowly, like Greenbach was looking for a turn. I bumped the Buick across a rail-crossing, a freight train hauling rusted metal trucks a hundred yards away.

I must have ignored a red signal somewhere because the engineer gave me three derisive blasts on his klaxon. I was too busy minding my own business and I accelerated up to keep Greenbach in sight. It was a depressing industrial area, the buildings looking bleached in the harsh light, like they'd been dusted with powdered cement. Grit and smog stung my eyelids and two silver chimneys belched acrid yellow fumes into the suffering sky.

I caught up a little but I didn't want to get too close in this deserted area so I kept an even pace. The road seemed to be giving out in a desert of decaying warehouses, vacant lots, dumps of rotting debris and old rusted girders. The springs of the Buick groaned ominously at the pot-holes but I could see Greenbach's vehicle way ahead so I kept on going.

I came out on an area of rock thick with dust where the blown plumes of Greenbach's passage still hung on the air. There were five roads radiating from it like the spokes of a wheel. I got out in the middle when there was a sudden crack. I thought the springs had gone but the windscreen suddenly starred close to my head.

Reflex action drove me down below window level, my foot stabbing the accelerator pedal. The heavy duty truck with tyres as big as a tank track screamed out of a side-turn between two concrete buildings. My own tyres bit as they tore at the rock and then I was careering forward down the narrow track between scrubland as the blank snout of the truck radiator loomed as big as a house in my rear mirror.

8

Tyres screamed on rock as the Buick jolted down the track at a suicidal pace. I spun the wheel, dust blurring the starred windscreen. Somehow I kept the automobile on the level though I felt the two nearside wheels leave the ground as we went over some big rocky obstruction. I could see the truck slewed at a crazy angle in the rear mirror which was juddering so hard I thought it was going to go through the Buick's roof.

I gritted my teeth and hung on. You've had worse, Mike, I told myself as another report sounded over the roar of the motor. The marksman's aim must have been off because I couldn't see any further damage to the screen and nothing hit the body. The dusty track ahead was just a blur and Greenbach's heap had long disappeared.

Another stone building was coming up on the right and I slewed and got behind it, dust drifting across the track. I could hear the truck tyres scream and then the heavy grinding of gears as the driver changed down. Brakes squealed and I got my head up and shot a quick glance in the mirror. The truck had missed the turn and was stalled. It clumsily backed as I cut through some scrubland, gaining thirty yards where the rock road made an S across the landscape.

I was looking for an angle but I couldn't find one. There was nothing basically wrong with the Buick except the damaged screen but I couldn't afford to let the truck catch up with me. My heap was no match for the massive, tank-like body in a duel. Equally, there was no future in abandoning the car and trying to escape on foot in this terrain. It was just a short-cut to suicide. I glanced back out the side window. The truck was nowhere in sight but it could only be seconds before it re-appeared.

Some tips were coming up now; they looked like refuse heaps and fires were burning here and there, making the place resemble Vesuvius. That is, Vesuvius on its day off. The surroundings here couldn't compete with the Bay of Naples. I skirted the first tip and got the Buick off the road, jolting and bucking across the uneven ground. I caught a glimpse of the big truck then, coming over a rise several hundred yards away, before the streamers of smoke blotted me out.

If I could find a way back on to the main stem from here I might stand a chance. I didn't think the truck operators had anyone else with them. If they had I'd have seen evidence of it before. Even the truck alone was formidable enough. But the truck and an automobile would soon have me boxed in. I looked at the fuel gauge. I had a three-quarter full tank. No problems there.

I spun the wheel again, the tyres making heavy vibrations over the rough ground; a flimsy wooden hut, its broken windows showing like blackened teeth in the sunlight, slid by on my right. A man in dungarees ran from the door, his mouth a dark gash of surprise in his face. His cry was lost in the roar of the engine and then I was snaking the Buick crazily between the smoking dumps, tin cans and other loose debris rattling and clattering away from underneath the tyres.

I caught only a glimpse in the rear mirror but the big truck was already gaining; in the fractional moment of stillness between vibrations, when the Buick was at the top of a curve and before it hit ground again with a bone-shuddering crash, I saw the snout of the truck catch the side of the hut. It went flat like a cardboard cut-out and the massive wheels of the truck crushed and scattered the debris. The figure in overalls went rolling away, his hands over his head and then I took my eyes from the mirror, fighting the wheel and the steering, trying to keep control of the automobile's crazy gyrations.

I went in and out the tips like an Olympic skier doing a slalom and somehow managed to avoid any major collision with the old car bodies, rusty oil drums and other obstructions with which the area was littered. For a brief moment I looked in the mirror again and saw the truck had disappeared. Then I heard the thunder of the diesel over the noise of my own engine.

The big truck had cut across the open ground instead of taking off after me. I spun the wheel, did a shrieking U-turn that had my heart somewhere up near my nostrils and my nerves dancing like ping-pong balls. As I straightened I forced the Buick back over the mouldering refuse in a direction parallel to that which I had already traversed.

At the same moment there was a cracking roar and a cloud of dust like a miniature Hiroshima. The big truck had turned at right angles parallel to my course and had simply gone straight through the tip, scattering ashes and debris in all directions. The machine was tilted at an incredible angle and for a moment, as I craned back over my shoulder, I thought he wasn't going to make it. But the wheelman must have been a top pro because he slewed sideways to the left and went on.

He'd obviously expected to hit me broadside or come out close on my tail.

If I had continued on course he would undoubtedly have side-swiped me. Now, not only had he missed me but he was facing in the wrong direction. I grinned and put my toe down, watching him recede in the mirror. I got back to the crushed watchman's hut in time to meet the character in coveralls who'd just gotten up.

He threw himself in the other direction and went rolling down a bank littered with empty coca-cola cans as my bonnet shaved his rump. I was sorry about it but I'd had a job enough to miss him as it was. This was no time for the finer points of driving etiquette. I was still looking for an angle but I couldn't come up with one.

I zigzagged between some derelict tar-paper sheds with sagging roofs. I took the Smith-Wesson out my holster and laid it down on the passenger seat next me where I could get at it easily.

I hadn't had time to get off a shot yet but if I could meet him head on I'd stand a good chance. The terrain would have to be right though; otherwise he would merely ram me. If I hit the driver that wouldn't stop a truck of that weight and size. Unless I had plenty of room to manoeuvre it would simply keep coming and crush me. I shook the sweat out of my eyes. I'd only use the Smith-Wesson as a last resort.

I was going down a slope now, over a firm, rocky surface. I jammed on the brakes. Now that I was halfway down I could see it led into a sort of quarry with high, unclimbable rock walls. The area was half-filled with rotting debris which had silted down from above. It was obviously an overflow area from the tips, where dumpers simply reversed to the edges and let go their loads.

I was sweating as I started to turn around. I got the bonnet up to the rocky wall on the right-hand side of the entrance ramp and put the Buick into reverse. I was clumsy with the lever and she stalled. I re-started the engine and eased back from the wall. I completed the manoeuvre and gunned back up the ramp expecting to see the silhouette of the big truck charging down on me. My hands were trembling very slightly as I crested the ridge.

★ ★ ★

The truck wasn't yet in sight. I idled up over the crest and turned right, into a sort of alley bounded on one side by a shed with a tar-paper roof and on the other by thousands of empty beer-cans, evidently the spillage from the vast tip which towered up to about eighty feet. The shed had an open end. I had an idea then. I drove the Buick swiftly in and got out. I ran quickly back to the open end of the shed.

I could faintly hear the throbbing of the truck diesel but it was evidently a fair way off. I ran down the side of the shed, holding the Smith-Wesson ready in my hand. I was taking a hell of a risk but I had to check on something. It was the only thing I could think of on the spur of the moment. The end of the shed was composed only of loose boards held on battens. The whole thing sagged as I put my hand against it.

More important still was the set-up behind it. At the back of the shed was a clear area of rocky shelf about twenty feet wide. It led back to the track which wound its way to the industrial area from which I'd just come. The rock shelf was bounded by a high board fence. I examined this quickly. There were big splits in it. Beyond, a mere two feet, was a thirty-feet drop to the floor of a quarry.

I went back to the shed, conscious now of the rumble of the truck motor becoming more audible. There was no time to get round the front. I pulled at the boards, oblivious of the harsh scream of rusty nails as I levered them back. I was sweating again by the time I made a big hole. I stepped in through to the interior of the shed and pulled the board back behind me. I got behind the wheel of the Buick and re-started the motor.

As I did that I heard the harsh roar of the truck and the ground trembled as it thundered by. It went straight down the ramp which led to the empty quarry. I could hear the hissing of air-brakes and the scream of tyres. I grinned. I might stand a fair chance now. I quietly put the Buick in reverse until I was right back across the alley, the nose of my car facing into the empty shed.

I sat there, my nerves crawling, listening to the screaming noises as the truck-driver reversed the huge machine on the narrow sloping ramp. I hoped he'd be going slowly when he reached the mouth of the alley. I wanted him to see me and follow. I put the Smith-Wesson back on the seat beside me and sat looking toward the alley entrance. The rumble of the truck was coming nearer.

I saw its snout start to pass the end of the alley, the scream of the brakes coming a second later. I gunned up the engine. The driver hadn't bothered to stop; he kept on going, hauling at the wheel, the heavy steel girders on the front of the bonnet tearing the side out of one of the wooden buildings on the lot. The truck looked like the QE2 as it charged toward me. Sweat ran down my face. I had to gauge it carefully.

It was about six yards away when I

let in the gear and rocketed across the alley into the open end of the big shed opposite. The hiss of the truck brakes seemed to split my skull but I kept on going. Beer-cans sprayed into the air as the heavy duty vehicle ground on, the driver pulling round. In the mirror I could see the truck was so bulky it filled the whole of the end of the shed. For one second I thought it was so tall it would pull the whole structure in on me but it just cleared.

I slewed the wheel and put the Buick at the planking; it tore out like a rotten apple and then I was through into the open air beyond, my tyres tearing at the rocky shelf. For a second or so I thought I'd miscalculated but I just managed to pull round, leaving the board fence masking the quarry a couple of feet to my right. There was another crash as the truck took the end of the shed out.

It was so big it was almost on the fence before the driver could turn. I knew he hadn't a hope in hell of making it so I braked and started drawing up. I looked back as the big steel crash-bars took a whole ten-feet section of fencing out in one neat bite. The section wheeled into space below, seemingly in slow-motion. I could hear the thin screams clear over the roar of the motor as the truck arced out into the void.

It sailed silently down to the quarry floor. The impact seemed to shake the ground where I sat in the Buick and the explosion as the tank went up sent tongues of orange flame and acrid black smoke a hundred feet into the air. I got out the Buick, leaving the motor running, and ran back. I looked down at the white-hot pyre on the quarry floor and turned away. There was nothing I could do.

As I got in the Buick the big character in coveralls appeared round the edge of the fence. His face was white and blenched with fear. He gaped at the column of fire.

"Jeezechrise, Jeezechrise," he said over and over again under his breath.

He licked his lips and put his hand on the edge of my driving door.

"What the hell's going on?"

"A home-made cremation," I told him. "You'd better get some law in."

I gunned up the engine and left him there. I turned right at the board fence, found the track by which I'd come in and got the hell out.

9

"Nice going, Mike," Stella said.

She gave me a wry smile as she sat on the edge of her desk, swinging a long, shapely leg. "You could say that," I said. "Or then again you could argue that I came out on top."

Stella smiled. I could have watched it all day.

"There is that," she said gently. "Coffee?"

"Try me," I said.

She went over to the glassed-in alcove where we do the brewing-up with long, athletic strides. She had a nice action. I'd always admired it and this occasion was no exception. She was built like a Swiss precision watch.

Stella frowned at me from round the alcove like she could figure what I was thinking.

"You have a disgusting leer on your face, Mike. Knock it off."

"That's my transparent honesty, honey," I said. "It's part of my charm."

Stella gave an elegant snort.

"It's just plain lechery where I come from," she said.

"We're not where you come from," I said.

Stella didn't answer that. She stood fooling around with crockery and percolators while I concentrated on the cracks in the ceiling and sat salivating like one of Pavlov's dogs while the aroma of freshly roasted coffee beans began to permeate the office. Stella came back, leaned against her desk and folded her arms.

"So what did these characters want, Mike?"

I shrugged.

"They could be the people Dillon hired me to protect Greenbach from. Or somebody else is interested in Greenbach too."

Stella wrinkled up her forehead. Her eyes looked very blue as she stood staring down at me.

"Or Greenbach could have his own

hired help who didn't like the tail Dillon put on him," she said.

I sat staring at her, giving her the frown back.

"It's a possibility," I said. "We got a lot of angles."

"None of it makes sense, though," Stella said. "Why all the interest in Greenbach?"

"He's an industrial chemist," I said. "Maybe he came up with some important process."

"Sure," Stella said. "Like the inexhaustible safety match or the car that runs on cabbage water."

I stared at Stella steadily.

"It's been done," I said. "Though it isn't so far-fetched. Why else would they try to stop me tailing him?"

Stella went back over to the alcove without answering. I sat listening to the clinking of cups and watching the watery afternoon sunlight fading the threadbare carpet in my office. From the boulevard below came the muted roar of the stalled traffic. The plastic fan kept pecking at what was left of the silence. I could have

101

done with a vacation right now. Dillon's commission was something I could have done without.

Stella came back and put the coffee on my blotter, slid the sugar bowl over. Just then the phone buzzed. Stella was halfway back from the alcove with her own cup. The phone went on buzzing. She looked at me reproachfully.

"Don't exhaust yourself."

"It's the weather," I said. "Besides, the phone is just out of reach. The cleaning-woman always leaves it too far over."

Stella looked at me pityingly. She put down her coffee and picked up the receiver.

"Faraday Investigations. Yes, he is. Just a moment."

She cupped the mouthpiece and turned to me.

"Dillon."

I sighed.

"There goes my coffee break."

I clawed my own instrument over.

"Dillon here, Faraday. Just checking out."

I grunted.

"I wanted to see you."

"Something happened?"

Dillon's voice sounded edgy.

"Just routine," I said. "Two characters tried to rub me. Looks like you've got some explaining to do."

"I don't understand you."

Dillon had control of himself now. There was a hard ring to his voice.

"You understand all right," I said. "I want to know more about this assignment. I was tailing Greenbach last night when someone tried to side-swipe me with a heavy duty truck."

There was a heavy silence from the other end like Dillon was thinking. Stella looked at me brightly and tapped gently with her gold pencil on a row of perfect white teeth.

"You lost Greenbach?"

"Sure I lost Greenbach," I said. "But that was better than losing my life."

"Sure," Dillon said. "I didn't mean anything by that. Naturally."

"Naturally," I said. "The heavies in the truck crashed and burned. You'll see it in the evenings."

"Christ," Dillon said helplessly.

"He can't help," I told him. "Like I said I need more information. I'll look by within the hour. You going to be there?"

"I'll be here," Dillon said heavily.

He put the phone down.

I looked at Stella.

"Something phoney here," she said. "You already checked with Dillon yesterday."

I smiled at her.

"Good reasoning, honey. Just what I thought."

Stella frowned.

"Dillon knew about the set-up?"

I shook my head.

"Sounds unlikely. But like he said he was expecting some sort of attempt on Greenbach's life. Why hire me otherwise? Maybe the truck was trailing Greenbach and I got in the way."

"Maybe," Stella said cautiously. "Anyway you'll know a little more after you see Dillon."

"Want to bet?" I said. "Dillon strikes me as slightly less loquacious than a

104

well-known shellfish."

Stella grinned.

"Another cup?"

"Hit me again," I told her.

I waited until she came back.

"Something I overlooked," I said. "Those TV programmes."

Stella shook her head.

"I got to it," she said. "I did a rundown for you. It's on the desk here."

She handed me several printed sheets; they were the local and national TV schedules. She'd ringed relevant items in ink correlating with the time I'd been outside Greenbach's window.

"Jesus," I said. "They were watching this stuff?"

"If they were they must have been in their second childhood," she said.

I squinted at the schedules again. Apart from the chat shows, the quizzes and the asinine family situation comedies there was only an Indians v Cavalry feature film which had hit the big screens at least thirty-five years before.

"Prime time," said Stella, putting the cup down on my blotter.

"You can say that again," I said.

"When will your car be ready?" Stella said.

"Tea-time," I said. "They're putting a new screen in."

I flipped the sheets away and sat looking at the shimmer of the overhead light glinting on the dark surface of the coffee. It seemed about as murky and foreboding as the whole case so far. I stopped beating my brains out and gave it up.

* * *

It was around a quarter of eight when I got to the Astor Bar. It was crowded like always and there was no sign of the girl. I ordered a beer and carried it to an empty booth up at one end. I set fire to a cigarette and watched the people round about. It was pretty crowded and there was a lot of noise, drowning out the muzak that dribbled from the concealed speakers.

It was a quarter after eight before she showed. She looked more striking than ever. It was warm again tonight. The sun had been shining after heavy rain so that now it was dark the streets were dry and fresh-smelling. Maybe because of the warmth she favoured the cream linen suit with the red silk scarf and the leather toggle. She carried a white matching raincoat over her arm and came swinging down the bar with a lithe step that caused a lot of turned heads. Mine felt like it was on a swivel itself.

She showed a line of pure white as she eased her face into a faint smile.

"Waiting long?"

"Just long enough," I said.

She raised her eyebrows.

"Meaning what?"

"Just long enough to be interested," I said. "Not long enough to be irritated."

She laughed, smoothing back her hair with a brown hand and sliding into a seat opposite me in the booth.

"It's a fine distinction."

The steady grey eyes were no longer haughty as she looked at me curiously. The white-jacketed waiter was already over to the table before she had settled herself on the banquette. I glanced at him frostily. I could have sat there half an hour without getting the same service.

The girl ordered a gin-fizz and I settled for another beer. The drinks were on the table before she spoke again, raising the glass ironically in a toast.

"Would you like dinner somewhere?" I said.

She shook her head.

"I've already eaten. But we can take a walk later."

I stared at her.

"In L.A. in the dark?"

She shook her head, passing a pink tongue over the white teeth.

"We could drive to the beach. It's a beautiful night now."

"Sure," I said. "If you want."

I put down my glass on the table, staring through the thin smoke at the rest of the people in the room.

"Do you often do it?"

The girl shifted on the banquette, cupping brown hands round the stem of her glass.

"Do what?" she said.

"Walk on the beach," I said. "Alone, I mean."

"Sometimes," she said. "With a friend occasionally. Mostly alone."

"Aren't you afraid?" I said.

The girl looked genuinely surprised.

"Of what?"

"Muggers or worse," I said. "The beach can be a dangerous place at night."

Della Strongman smiled.

"They don't worry me," she said. "It's too far out where I go. And in any event I can hold my own just fine. I took a course in judo."

I grinned.

"That makes two of us."

The cool grey eyes appraised me frankly.

"Should be an interesting stroll, Mike."

It was the first time she had used my name.

I lit a cigarette at the Strongman number's tacitly extended permission.

"Delectable as the evening promises to be," I said. "You didn't intend this to be entirely a social occasion?"

The girl's eyelids fluttered. Whether with amusement or disdain I couldn't make out.

"You're a pretty good private-eye," she said.

"You'll crack my ego up if you go on ribbing me," I said.

The eyelids flickered again.

"I thought you were the strong, silent type who didn't fray at the edges."

"That's at week-ends," I said. "Tonight's a week-night and I'm not wearing my Y-fronts."

Della Strongman's façade almost shattered but she recovered herself in time. She was silent for a moment, frowning into her half-filled glass.

"There was something. I don't quite know how to approach it."

"Dillon's assignment?"

She nodded.

"There's something not quite right about it."

"You can say that again," I told her. "Your boss didn't exactly strike me as being forthcoming."

She picked up her glass and finished off her drink as though she'd come to a decision.

"You want another?"

She shook her head.

"Maybe this place is too public," she said.

"Meaning what?"

"Meaning we've got things to talk about, Mike."

"Dillon know you're here?" I said.

She shook her head and got up from the table.

"I keep my life in separate compartments. There are one or two things about the Greenbach case I think you ought to know."

I gave her a long look.

"Information is something I could do with right now."

I finished my beer and stood up. She slipped her arm through mine.

"Let's talk on the beach," she said.

10

The Pacific made a thin white line in the dusk as cold-looking breakers tumbled in at the edge of the sand. The wind blew moist and fresh after the stickiness of the day and farther out the livid pencil of a lighthouse flecked the water briefly to a mauvy-green. The girl walked moodily toward the edge of the sea, scuffing her feet and leaving little crooked squiggles in the wet sand behind us.

"Who's watching Greenbach tonight?" she said.

"A good question," I told her. "I called in to see Dillon late this afternoon. We had a rather heated conversation."

It was too dark to see the girl's expression.

"About what?"

"About the assignment," I said. "I hinted in my subtle way that it was about time he opened up."

Della Strongman's teeth glinted whitely

in her face as she turned toward me. We were about a dozen yards from the water's edge now and the Pacific was making thin hissing noises, dragging runnels through the sand as it withdrew.

"He wouldn't like that."

"He didn't," I said.

The girl scuffed her foot in the sand again like she was thinking heavily.

"You want to tell me about it?"

"There's no reason why you shouldn't know," I said. "Two characters in a truck tried to kill me yesterday when I was tailing Greenbach. There was an item in tonight's paper so it's public property."

The girl's face was a grey blur above the white raincoat in the semi-darkness. She drew her breath in with a little explosive sound.

"That's bad, Mike. What happened to Greenbach?"

"He had already disappeared when they showed up," I said.

Della Strongman turned her face to the moonlight so that I could read the expression in her eyes.

"Dillon wouldn't like that," she said again.

"Neither did I," I told her. "No one else but you and Dillon and my secretary know that I was there, of course. It's got to stay that way. For the time being, that is."

The girl put up her hand to brush the hair from her eyes.

"Of course. Any ideas? On why they should want to kill you?"

I shook my head.

"Lots of ideas but no facts. I was hoping you might help. You said you had something to tell me about the assignment."

The girl walked on a little closer to the edge of the sea, looking at the tumbling runnels of foam as though they held the answer to her thoughts. I followed, dodging round deep pools of salt water left by the receding tide.

"It will keep for a minute, Mike. How did things finish up with Dillon?"

"Inconclusively," I said. "I told him he could stuff his assignment and then came away."

114

The girl gave a little gurgle of amusement.

"That would be quite a novelty for Dillon," she said.

"It was," I said. "Anyway, I got a call as soon as I arrived back at the office. He'd cooled down. I'm back on the case. Such as it is. I checked on Greenbach but he was nowhere around."

"It makes no matter," said the Strongman number calmly. "He had an appointment to meet Dillon tonight."

"That's what Dillon said," I told her. "So I took the evening off."

The girl was silent again like something was troubling her and we had walked a quarter of a mile before she spoke again.

"Dillon told you, of course, that Greenbach had been threatened. What he didn't tell you was the cause."

I stared at her for a long moment.

"You know the cause?"

"Not exactly, but it's some sort of new chemical process that's worth a lot of money. A much cheaper method of refining petrol with an additive that gives twice the mileage per gallon."

"How do you know all this?" I said.

The girl's eyes flickered.

"I found some papers on Dillon's desk once. Stuff I wasn't supposed to see. I put them back and said nothing. But when he hired you I put two and two together."

"And came up with five," I said. "There's something still doesn't jell. If Greenbach's come up with something for his firm surely they would give him police protection if his life were threatened. An invention like that's too big to keep under tabs."

Della Strongman shrugged.

"Maybe, Mike."

"You don't think so?" I said.

"Perhaps his firm doesn't know," she said. "Suppose the thing was developed off their time. And he's up for the highest bidder."

"You got a point," I conceded. "But that still doesn't explain why I'm tailing Greenbach without his knowledge."

The girl shook her head.

"You don't know Greenbach, Mike. He's a pure scientist and a man entirely

116

without fear. His personal safety wouldn't weigh with him one scrap. And he's totally careless of his own safety."

"So Dillon is protecting his interests?" I said.

"Sort of," Della Strongman countered. "I know he's got shares in some of Greenbach's industrial enterprises."

"So where does the blonde number come in?" I said.

The girl laughed.

"Greenbach's got a number of those, Mike."

She held up her hand.

"No, not for the reason you think. He pays them very well and they act as high-class secretaries. They have to be on call day and night for his various enterprises."

"That's a new one," I said.

"It's the truth, Mike. The good doctor doesn't seem to have any sexual interests at all."

"It takes all sorts," I said.

Della Strongman had stopped, her back to the ocean, the stippled moonlight breaking in bars of silver and black behind her strands of flying hair.

"Thanks a lot," I said. "You've given me something to think about. You're sure that's everything?"

The girl started scuffing her foot again.

"I think so, Mike. But if I come up with anything else I'll give you a call. When do you pick up Greenbach again?"

"First thing in the morning," I said.

★ ★ ★

It was nearly midnight when I left the girl. I had a lot to think about as I drove away. I caught the 12 o'clock bulletin and killed a couple of minutes. Then I turned the Buick and tooled on over toward the edge of town. It was early yet for what I had in mind.

It began raining as I flipped the radio off and I started the wipers, looking through the cleared wedge of glass at the tropical foliage that was being spoiled by the downpour. After a few minutes it really started and I slackened speed. I had a job to see what with the grit on the windshield and the sludge thrown up by the slip-streams of other cars. Neon glinted green, gold and mauve through the wet, turning the glaucous surface of the road into the semblance of a tropical fish-tank.

I found the turn for Laurel Canyon and it was around half-past twelve when I pulled up a hundred yards from the Spanish-style property. The rain had slackened a little but it was still bombarding the broad-leaved foliage and driving shoals of grit down the storm-drains as I gum-shoed over the shaved lawns and up to the entrance.

There were no lights on anywhere but I made it up to the garage and peeked in through the side-windows. There was enough light coming from the street-lamps to see that the interior was empty. I went back to the Buick, dragged myself behind the wheel and lit a cigarette. There were several other cars parked up ahead so I wasn't too conspicuous. I hadn't got my raincoat this evening so I was pretty wet by this time and none too happy with the set-up.

I hadn't been sitting there more than fifteen minutes before there came the hum of a motor and headlamp beams stencilled stripes of yellow across the rear windows of my heap. I got down in my seat and watched as a scarlet station-wagon turned into the entrance to Greenbach's property. It growled up to the garage and the up-and-over doors operated automatically as the interior lights came on. The wagon eased inside and then I heard the car-doors slam.

From where I was sitting I could see the garage lights through a flowering hedge but without much detail. I saw two shadows pass across the light. A few seconds later the doors slid shut and the light went out. I was out the car this time, my footsteps masked by the thin patter of the falling rain. The porch-light went on as I got up on the smooth turf that bordered the garage drive.

A man was putting his key in the door. It was Greenbach all right. The bald head with the fringe of black hair was unmistakable. The tall blonde was there too. She wore white tailored slacks and a short leather jacket. She was facing toward me as she waited for her companion to open the door. I waited until they'd gone inside before I moved.

I got under the shelter of a tree as the porch-light went out. I looked round carefully. There was a hedge sheltering me from the road but there was too much light here for my liking. I walked up the lawn as the house-lights went on. I worked my way around in back. I gave them twenty minutes to get settled down.

It was one-fifteen a.m. before I made my move and I was damp and bored. The house sat there looking at me, calm and hospitable with the yellow lights in the windows.

I got out from under the tree and walked up the edge of the lawn that bordered the cement path that led to the back stoop. I was halfway along it when four shots blammed out so quickly that they sounded almost like one.

11

I swore, reaching for the Smith-Wesson. I had it out, my feet beating a tattoo on the path as I flung myself at the back-door. It was locked, like I figured, but the flimsy glass construction shattered as I put my shoulder to it and I went through in a shower of splinters and breaking glass that would have made Burt Lancaster green with envy.

The lights were on in the back hallway and my rush carried me on through into the living room. Another shot sounded then, much louder than the others and I went down as the light fitting above my head shattered. I crawled away through the shadow beyond the open doorway into the corridor. There was a black and white marble tiled floor in the living room which was so big it seemed to stretch away into infinity.

There were two massive standard lamps set each side a green leather divan that was all of twenty feet long. They were set to illuminate the great stone and timber fireplace in French Provençal style that was set over against the left-hand wall. The far end of the room was still in shadow and the unfriendly character who'd taken a shot at me was obviously holed up somewhere there.

I crawled farther into the wall. I'd already thrown the safety off the Smith-Wesson and I poked the barrel round the edge of the door-lintel at floor level. Slight as the movement was it attracted attention. I drew swiftly back. The shot was so accurate that the slug chipped a long groove in the marble flooring, the chips whining angrily about the corridor. I closed my eyes, feeling dust and grit stinging my cheeks. The gun-artist must have had fantastic eye-sight.

He'd got all the advantages on his side too. He was in shadow but the divan lights illuminated the doorway like I was on a stage. That's why he'd got the overhead light fitting in the hall. He'd aimed to do that so that he could concentrate on the black oblong of the door. I decided to even the odds. I carefully crawled back a yard or so and got to my feet. I went back down the corridor, keeping well away from the direct range of the open door.

I got about fifteen feet away and found the edge of the first standard lamp coming up on the left-hand side of the door. I got off a snap-shot and jumped back into the shadow. The heavy crack drew another shot from the heavy but the sudden pool of darkness on the near side of the room showed I'd achieved my objective.

There was no sense in hanging about. I took a deep breath and lined up on the doorway. Good luck, Mike, I told myself. I went through into the living room so fast I must have looked like a blur. Fear accelerated me more than anything else. I dived into the welcome blackness beneath the divan, oblivious of the broken glass that was littering the carpet. I heard another bang and then a crash but the slug went a long way wide because plaster rained from the wall.

I kept rolling and pumped off another

couple into the blackness at the far end of the room. The muzzle-flashes seemed to light the place up. Glass tinkled in rear and a heavy body blundered about. Then a door slammed and I heard running footsteps on the cement path outside. As I got to the French door a car gunned up in front of the house. I grinned crookedly and went back into the living room.

I found another switch up near the fireplace and buttoned it. The overhead lights came on. The place looked only slightly less better than the San Francisco earthquake. I went over to a bar at the side of the room, found a bottle of bourbon and gave myself a stiff shot. I knew what I was going to find and felt I needed it.

When I'd steadied myself up a little I went back over to the windows, bolted them and drew the thick drapes. I waited, the seconds crawling by, but there was no further sound from outside. The house was a long way back from the road and most probably no-one in neighbouring houses had heard anything.

But I hung on to make sure. I didn't

want to be found here under these circumstances if I could avoid it. When I was certain I wouldn't be disturbed I went over to the middle of the room. The phone jangled while I was doing that. The sound seemed to sear my nerves like acid. I let it ring. The noise still scalding my concentration I went over behind the divan. The two bodies were lying asprawl, their arms outstretched.

There was surprisingly little blood. Greenbach had been hit at least twice. The long black fringe of hair about his bald crown was plastered like seaweed across his forehead and down his swarthy features. The perspiration was still glistening on his skin and a thin trickle of black blood ran out the corner of his mouth and across his chin to spread over his white silk shirt. The red bowtie was stained a darker colour. The phone had stopped ringing now.

Greenbach's eyes were wide and surprised, the mouth open in a rictus which exposed the perfect teeth in a goodbye smile. I found two bullet wounds in the chest, fairly close together. I lifted his lapels carefully, leafed through his billfold. It was Greenbach all right; his driver's licence told me that but I wanted to make certain.

I'd been on an assignment once when the man I was tailing got shot. He'd turned out to be someone entirely different from what I'd been told by my client. It made me look foolish and I'd never forgotten it. I went through the wallet; there was plenty of money in there; about five or six hundred dollars in high denomination bills; diner's club cards; membership documents for a number of learned institutions; and an identity card for entry to Arnos Chemicals complex.

There was no photograph with it, just the name and address typed in. I took the card and put the rest of the stuff back in his wallet as I'd found it. Then I slid the wallet in his breast-pocket and the identity card in mine. I might want to get into Arnos Chemicals some time and it could come in useful.

I heard a strange whistling sound. It made the flesh on the back of my neck crawl. A slim white hand was twisting across the divan toward me. I got to the girl's body and turned her gently over. The blonde number had an ashen face. There was a lot of blood on the front of her leather jacket, low down; I winced as I looked at the damage. A stomach wound was bad at any time but this looked one of the worst kind.

I made her comfortable with cushions, got a clean handkerchief from Greenbach's breast pocket, made a pad of it and using my own as a topper stanched the wound as best I could. The blonde girl's eyelids flickered and a small tear trickled down to the corner of her mouth. Her eyes were expressing intelligence now, though the pupils were clouded with pain. I put down my head close to her lips.

"Hugo's dead?"

I nodded.

"Don't worry. You'll be all right."

I left her and went over to the phone, dialled the emergency ambulance service and told them where to come. When I went back to the girl I found her raised slightly, her eyes fixed on Greenbach's body. I knelt in front of her so she couldn't see. The white slacks were no longer white. Despite the greyness of her complexion she still looked a beautiful woman. Her eyes flickered and I guessed rather than heard her ask me to come closer.

I bent low, conscious of her cloying perfume and the warm breath on my cheek.

"Case," she said. "Get case."

Her eyes turned upward. I got up, soon saw what she meant. A black leather briefcase was jammed down the divan back, almost invisible among the cushions. I pulled it out, found the key in the lock. Looked like they'd been about to open it when the hatchet-man struck. Greenbach or the girl must have stuffed it down the divan just before the shooting started. That meant it had to be important. I held it up in front of the girl.

"This what you meant?"

She smiled, passed out before she finished it. Her head lolled over. I felt her pulse. It was still weak but she'd only fainted. I looked at my watch. Another ten minutes had gone by. I couldn't afford to hang around. The ambulance boys would be hitting any minute.

I carefully unbuckled the girl's leather belt. Gently, I re-fixed it so as to hold the improvised handkerchief bandage in place. That would have to do until they got her to hospital. I re-loaded the Smith-Wesson and put it away. I saw then that a cabinet at the far side of the room had the doors open. It was partly in shadow and it wasn't until I got up to it that I saw it was a TV set. That gave me an idea but I had no time to work on it.

I went back out the place the same way I came in, carrying the briefcase and making sure I hadn't left any prints anywhere. I went down the cement path in front of the house without concealment, feeling like I was in the middle of a spotlight. The wind sighed in the tree-tops and the road was silent and deserted under the bloom of the street-lamps.

I slid behind the wheel of the Buick, started the motor and eased out. I had gone about three hundred yards when the headlights of a car parked about thirty feet from Greenbach's place flicked into life. I swore. It pulled out to follow as I accelerated away.

* * *

As soon as I had gone half a mile I made a right-angle turn down a side-lane. The other car followed, making the same turn at a sedate pace. It was a big, anonymous-looking black sedan. I figured it was a back-up car for the gun-artist. It took some nerve. They'd stayed put when the killer got out. And they knew I'd got the briefcase. I looked at it on the seat beside me, my mind revolving like the cylinders in a fruit-machine.

I got out the Smith-Wesson and laid it down next the briefcase. I was at an intersection leading back to the mainstem now. I waited until the lights changed to green. The black sedan kept well back, pulled away smoothly like it was linked to me with invisible thread. I felt a little better then. They didn't know me. They wanted to see where I was going.

131

I decided to make for the office. Their heap was more powerful than mine and I had no chance of shaking them. All the while they were content to follow I'd play it their way. Besides, I knew my building and they didn't. There'd be more chance to shake them. I turned things over in my mind for another couple of minutes. I didn't want to involve the night-porter.

I often worked all hours and he was used to me turning up sometimes in the middle of the night. Maybe I could send him out for a take-away meal if the characters in the sedan followed me into the building. I'd have to play it by ear. Usually, I leave the Buick in the underground garage I use, about two blocks away from my building but tonight I decided to park outside the main entrance.

There were no restrictions this time of the morning and by the time they'd parked I aimed to be well up toward my officer floor. I kept on driving steadily across town, but every time I turned off at an intersection the black sedan turned too; and whenever I halted at lights it kept well back, letting other vehicles overtake.

By the time I got to my building there was no possible doubt about the matter. The lighting wasn't very good but so far as I could make out in the necessarily hurried glimpses I got in the mirror, there were three silhouettes in the other car. Three men. The odds were too heavy for me to try anything fancy.

I thought things over for another minute or two. Then I reached for the Smith-Wesson, put the safety on and put it back in the holster. I pulled the briefcase toward me. I was only a few blocks from my office now. I made a turn before I got to it and circled. That way I'd be on the wrong side of the road. I looked in the mirror. There was nothing else behind me but the sedan for the moment.

I drove up toward my building, keeping in the fast lane, like I was going on past. The dark vehicle was fairly close now. I slackened speed. There was nothing coming but a couple of cars in the far distance, looking to be fast. I accelerated up like I'd suddenly remembered something and made a right turn into the opposing traffic, making my signal at the last minute.

I grinned as the car coming toward me gave me a blast of the horn. He was too close now for the sedan to follow. I pulled in in front of my building, killing the lights. I was facing in the wrong direction but it wouldn't matter unless a prowl car spotted my heap. I didn't want any interruption now. I wanted to find out who was so interested in Greenbach. I scooped up the briefcase and pulled out the ignition keys from the dash.

The sedan had had to go on because of the oncoming traffic flow. I grinned as I saw the rear light flashing for a right-hand turn at the next block. I would have at least a minute's start, maybe two. I crossed the sidewalk at a run. There was no-one in the lobby and the elevator wasn't working this time of the morning. I took the stairs two at a time, the briefcase making a hard pressure against my side.

I got up to the first floor. There

was no sign of the night-porter. Maybe he'd gone down to the basement for a smoke. I hoped he wouldn't show. I got up another two floors and stopped. There were dim lights burning in the corridors. I stopped and leaned against the wall, getting my breath. My heart was thumping unpleasantly and perspiration was trickling down inside my shirt-collar.

I heard the noise of a car pulling up in front of the building then. The squeal of the brakes was so loud it cut clear through the hum of the distant traffic. I hadn't got much time. I broke out the Smith-Wesson, threw off the safety and put it down on a window ledge near me, where I could get at it in a hurry. Then I opened the briefcase. I soon saw where the weight had been coming from. I blinked. I took out the black box with the trailing flex and plug. So far as I could make out it was the TV remote control switch Greenbach had been using the night I'd watched him and the girl through the window.

I could hear footsteps in the lobby now. They were slow and deliberate and they were coming clearly up the stair-well. I went through the rest of the contents of the briefcase quickly. There were some typed sheets of figures and numbers I couldn't make out. I folded those and put them in my trousers pocket. The rest of the stuff in the case looked like routine correspondence.

Most of it was on printed stationery, headed Arnos Chemicals. I stuffed it all back in the briefcase and closed it. I picked up the Smith-Wesson and padded quietly up another flight. I could hear footsteps coming up the stairs. I looked at the control box again. I had an obscure idea it might be important. Otherwise, why had the blonde number put such store by it? I hoped she'd make it. She was certainly a looker. And with any luck she'd be in hospital by now.

I had an idea then. There was a fire-bucket over near the elevator entrance. It was full of sand. I went over and stuffed the control box and flex down beneath the powdery surface. I worked fast, smoothing out the top to make like it hadn't been disturbed, careful not to spill any. When I had finished I could hear faint noises a flight below me. The hairs on the back of my neck were rising nicely now. I put a crushed cigarette pack on top of the sand in the bucket to make it look natural and stepped back.

When I was satisfied I crept up another flight, holding the briefcase in my left hand and the Smith-Wesson in my right. My heart was pumping a real treat now. I stopped in the shadow of the stairwell, listening to the footsteps. They went right past the area I'd just quitted without hesitation. These characters would know where my office was. Its location was on the board in the entrance hall, like always.

I had two more floors to go before my office. I didn't know what I intended to do. I didn't want to shoot it out, especially since I'd got rid of the important material in the case. But if I let it fall into their hands too easily they'd become suspicious. I thought of locking myself in and phoning Stella. Then I decided against. No reason to involve her.

I stood there, listening to the footsteps,

sweat trickling down the inside of my collar. I was still doing that, facing toward the stairwell when the fire-escape door in my rear opened with a squeak. I turned a mile too late, saw the figure in dark sweater and slacks. The stocking-mask looked like a sardonic death's head as the right leg came round, a blur in the dim light.

I brought the Smith-Wesson and the briefcase up together. The heavy leather took the impact of the shoe against my chin or the kick would have taken my head off. I blacked out and went down, losing all interest in the proceedings.

12

I tasted blood, groaned and found myself fully awake. My head was aching nicely and someone was playing Scott Joplin on my skull with an iron slicing bar. I opened my eyes, focused up. I was still lying in the shadow at the top of the stairwell. The Smith-Wesson was just beyond my outstretched hand. The briefcase was gone, of course. Just like I had intended. I tried to grin, stopped in case my jaw fell off.

I sat up, reaching tentatively for my chin. There was a lump there that felt the size of a pigeon's egg. I was functioning now. I went through my wallet and pockets. Nothing had been touched. Looked like the man in the mask had simply scooped up the briefcase without hanging around. Not that I blamed him. I checked the Smith-Wesson. The shells were in the chambers all right. I leaned back against the wall and sighed. It was a heavy case, in more ways than one.

I hesitated, started going down to the floor where I'd hidden the stuff in the fire-bucket, then decided against. They might still be hanging around and I'd had enough for one night. I went on up to my office, my feet feeling like lead, my skull giving out vibrations at every tread of the staircase. In the office I put on the lights, locked the door and drew the blinds.

I went in the wash-room and ran a cold water tap over my face and jaw. I found a half-empty bottle of bourbon in the drawer of my desk and helped myself to a shot. Still carrying the glass I went back into the wash-room and glanced at myself in the mirror.

To my surprise I looked almost human. My hair was dishevelled and my eyes heavy-lidded, but there was only a faint red and white mark at the side of my jaw. It would turn into a nice bruise later though. And I might have lost some teeth if I hadn't put the briefcase over my face.

I felt inside my mouth. I'd cut it on

one of my teeth. That's where the taste of blood had come from.

I put out the light and wandered back to my desk, unbuttoning my shirt. It wouldn't be worth going home now. I decided to grab some shut-eye on the divan in the corner. I'd wake at first light and go down and shift the Buick before the traffic started. I looked at my watch. It was almost three a.m. I took off my jacket, sat down on the divan and finished off the bourbon. I was asleep almost as soon as I got my feet off the floor.

I was awakened by the shrilling of the phone. It had just turned six a.m. The voice was Irish and friendly.

"Clancy here, Mr Faraday. I just spotted your heap. Everything all right?"

"Sure," I said. "I had a heavy night and forgot all about it."

He chuckled.

"Well, it's against the regulations, you know. You'd better move it before anybody important spots it."

"Thanks, Clancy," I said. "Be right down."

I put on my tie and my jacket and

walked down to the sidewalk. Clancy was leaning half-in, half-out his prowl car, listening moodily to the tinny voice of the radio spitting out instructions into the cool morning. I'd known him on and off for the last fifteen years and we'd done each other a few favours in our time.

He waved when I came up but didn't break off what he was doing so I got in the car, started her up and drove a couple of blocks to my usual car-park. I put the Buick in my permanent slot in the underground section and walked back up to my building. Clancy was already gone and the night-porter was nowhere to be seen but the power was on for the elevator so I buttoned myself up to my floor.

I got the electric razor from my desk and went back to the wash-room. I made a tolerable job of my stubble, then stripped to the waist and washed, soaping my face and body thoroughly with the chintzy tablet Stella had provided. I towelled myself vigorously and found my headache almost completely dispelled. There was a nice bump on my jaw, though, when I made a tentative exploration with my fingers.

I combed my hair, cleaned the wash-basin and replaced my shirt and tie. I went back out to the office, put my razor-set in my drawer and resumed my jacket. It was almost seven by now. I rode down again in the elevator, saw no-one and walked three blocks south to where there was a good coffee-shop. I got outside a decent breakfast and stopped beating my brains out.

* * *

Stella sat on a corner of the desk and looked at me sympathetically.

"You were lucky, Mike."

"You can say that again."

I put my feet up on my old broad-top and stared moodily at the cracks in the ceiling. Stella stopped swinging her leg and came over toward me.

"You ought to have that face seen to, Mike."

I looked at her but there didn't seem to be any irony in her voice.

Her fingers probed gently and experimentally along my jaw.

"Doesn't seem too bad," she said afterward. "A smallish bump but I should make sure."

"I'll look in and see the doc if the headache gets any worse," I said. "It's almost cleared."

"I seem to have heard that before," Stella said.

"It happens to be the truth in this case," I said. "And if you're asking me if I'd like coffee, you already know the answer."

Stella went over to the alcove and switched the percolator on. I sat and listened to the clinking of cups. She came back and stood looking down at me. She frowned at the sheets of figures and numbers on my blotter again.

"Some sort of code, Mike? But why?"

"You know as much as I do," I said.

"What about that gadget in the fire-bucket?"

I closed my eyes, listening to the steady pump of the blood in my veins.

"We'll leave it there for the time being," I said. "It's safe enough for the moment. And those characters might come back when they find the stuff in the briefcase is no use to them."

Stella shivered suddenly, like there was a draught in the room.

"I'm surprised Dillon hasn't been on. He just lost a client."

She answered my interrogatory stare.

"There was a flash on the radio early this morning. The girl's still hanging on. Looks like she might make it."

I stared at her in silence for a moment.

"I'm glad about that at any rate," I said. "She was a real looker."

I told her what Della Strongman had told me about the set-up. Stella went and got her scratchpad and jotted down the details. She stared at me thoughtfully, tapping with her gold pencil on very white teeth.

"This mess just gets messier, Mike."

"You have a point, honey," I agreed.

I waited for her to make the coffee. I was halfway through the first cup before she spoke again.

"What are you going to tell Dillon, Mike?"

"The truth," I said. "Leastways, all that's necessary for him to know."

I put up with her reproachful expression for thirty seconds longer.

"It is my licence, honey," I said. "And I've no intention of being bounced off it for a crummy assignment like Dillon's."

"Be fair, Mike," Stella said. "You could have been bounced off it for that truck episode the other day. And Dillon didn't say anything, did he?"

"Too true, he didn't," I said. "It's no more in his interest than mine to have the whole thing break in the press."

Stella went and sat on the edge of her own desk and sipped her coffee thoughtfully.

"Leastways, he can't blame you for this one, Mike. You were supposed to be off the assignment last night, remember?"

"I remember," I said. "It doesn't make me feel any better."

I took another swig of my coffee, reached out for the biscuit tin.

"Who was that girl, anyway?"

Stella's blue eyes were very cool and critical.

"The one who got shot with Greenbach? Zelda van Opper. Apparently a very ritzy young woman. A top secretary with the Zimmerman Agency. She was one of three hired out to Greenbach from time to time."

"That's what Della Strongman said," I told Stella. "So she was on the up and up."

"Any reason why she shouldn't be?" Stella said mildly.

"No reason," I said. "Except why should she be seen getting drunk at Garibaldi's that night I was tailing Greenbach. It wouldn't do anything for her image as a top secretary."

"Perhaps she was putting up a front," Stella said. "Acting on Greenbach's instructions."

I gave Stella a long, appraising look.

"You may have something there, honey. In which case the TV performance that night must have some significance that has so far escaped us. Otherwise, why would that control switch have been in the briefcase?"

Stella put down her cup with a faint clinking noise in the silence of the office.

"You want me to go down and get it, Mike?"

I shook my head.

"That's the last thing I want, honey. It's safe enough there."

"Unless the building catches fire," Stella said.

She had a curious look in her eyes.

"There is that," I conceded.

I drained the last of the coffee.

"Guess I'll go see Dillon," I said. "He might want to cry on my shoulder."

Stella smiled.

"That'll be the day," she said.

13

I walked a couple of blocks to my usual garage. The negro in the violent red shirt who seemed always to have worked there, was polishing a Cadillac and looking like he was putting his heart and soul into it. The brilliance of his smile lasted me all the way into the underground section.

There were only a few cars in here this time of day. I walked on down, listening to the melancholy drip of water into a bucket where someone had left a car-wash tap running. I stood admiring the Buick for a few seconds. They'd made a nice job of the new windshield. I was still standing there when I noticed another reflection had joined my own. It was that of a tall, slim man in a white drill suit.

When I turned around I saw that he was Chinese. It's difficult to figure age with Orientals; they always look so well-preserved into late middle-age, but I should have said he was around forty, though he looked a lot younger. He had a pale skin like he worked indoors a lot and his thick black hair was either lacquered or sprayed with some perfumed pomade. He stood looking at me, politely diffident, twisting his smart panama hat in his well-manicured hands.

"Mr Faraday?"

His voice was low and well-educated, without the trace of an accent.

"That's me," I said.

I glanced over his shoulder to an anonymous-looking pale blue Studebaker saloon. It was dim in here but I could faintly see three more Chinese sitting patiently in the interior. I glanced around but like always there was no-one else about in the vast underground concourse. The Chinese smiled encouragingly.

"Can you spare an hour or two, Mr Faraday?"

"I could," I said. "But not right now."

The man in the white suit smiled regretfully.

"My employer would like to see you right away, Mr Faraday. It would be to your advantage."

"Just who is your employer?" I said.

The Chinese shook his head.

"He prefers discretion, Mr Faraday."

"Does he," I said. "Your name?"

Again the polite smile.

"It wouldn't mean anything to you, Mr Faraday."

"And if I don't want to go?"

The smile broadened out another two millimetres. The Chinese shook his head.

"You don't strike me as being a foolish man, Mr Faraday. There are four of us and only one of you. This is a deserted place and I'm sure you don't want to use the gun in your pocket. After all, this is only a polite invitation."

I stood and traded smile for smile with him.

"You talked me into it," I said. "Providing we go in my heap."

The Chinese stepped back, an affable expression on his face. He nodded briefly to the three men. The engine of the Studebaker started up.

"For an Occidental you are very wise, Mr Faraday. I will ride with you. It will be necessary to blindfold you at one point. I take it you have no objection to my taking over the driving?"

"It will be safer than me carrying on with the blindfold," I said.

The Chinese bowed and stood back for me to get into the Buick.

"Allow me to congratulate you on your excellent sense of humour, Mr Faraday. It will be a pleasure to do business with you."

"That remains to be seen," I said.

The man in the white suit got in beside me, completely relaxed and at ease.

"I will give you instructions when we get across town," he said.

I switched on the engine, watching the Studebaker slide nearer in the rear mirror. The Chinese showed perfect white teeth as he smiled at me again.

"Let us drive, Mr Faraday."

I drove.

* * *

"I must apologize for the melodrama," the man in the white suit said.

"Think nothing of it," I told him.

The Chinese laughed.

"You are remarkably calm, Mr Faraday. One would imagine that this sort of situation is commonplace to you."

"It has happened before," I admitted.

I was sitting alongside him in the passenger seat of the Buick, a blindfold over my eyes. The ends of the heavy silk scarf dangled down and tickled my neck but I didn't want to put my hand up to scratch the irritation. I'd kept the Smith-Wesson. That was surprising in itself and I didn't want any action on my part to be misinterpreted.

It had been half an hour since we'd changed over and I was completely lost. There were just the usual traffic noises and once we'd stopped at lights. We were climbing steadily, about all I could make out. We hadn't gone to Chinatown, that was for sure. There was country air coming in through the window now, heavy with moisture and the perfume of flowers.

Presently the Buick pulled over on to gravel. Above the engine I could hear the noise of another. That would be the three men in the Studebaker. I sat with my hands folded in my lap, my body occasionally slumping as we turned curves. Then the noise of the engine was reverberating back against brick walls. We stopped and the motor cut out. The Chinese felt in my left-hand jacket pocket. He let go my bunch of keys and put his hand on my shoulder.

"We have arrived, Mr Faraday. I will guide you. Make no attempt to take off the bandage until I tell you."

I could hear dance-music now, faint and far away. It didn't seem to be coming from a radio. There was the unmistakable sound of real instruments, like it was a band playing in a ballroom.

I got out the car, White-suit's hand still on my shoulder. He'd gone around to the passenger door. Car doors slammed behind us. There was a hand on my elbow, steering me.

"There are some steps here. Be careful."

We walked up two flights. There was an elusive perfume in the air, like sandalwood. There was a heavy carpet beneath our feet and I could hear faint rustling movements, like women in heavy silks were nearby. It was an odd simile but it was all I could think of for the moment.

"We are turning right now, Mr Faraday. There are yet more steps. We are almost there."

"Tell me," I said. "It shouldn't be too difficult for me to find this place. A restaurant or road-house? Run by Chinese."

"My dear Mr Faraday."

My companion's voice was very urbane and patient.

"There are hundreds of Chinese establishments in the L.A. basin. What would be the point? You could, of course, make an effort in that direction. You might even trace this place with luck and determination. I sincerely advise you not to do so."

"Is that a threat?" I said.

"Good heavens no, Mr Faraday. People of great strength have no need of such crude tactics. I am merely concerned for your own good."

"Big organization?" I said.

The grip on my arm tightened.

"Right again and up another flight, Mr Faraday. To answer your last question, the biggest. But I am sure you will be sensible."

"I'm always sensible when it's in my own interest," I said. "It's natural to be curious about why I'm here."

"That I am not at liberty to tell you. But if you will be patient for another five minutes my employer will enlighten you."

We were up the last flight now and my guide paused. I heard him insert a key into a door-lock. Then the hand was on my elbow again and I was being ushered through the door. It closed behind us.

"You may remove the scarf now, Mr Faraday."

I did like he said, blinked in the light from the shaded lamps dotted around. I was in a large, panelled room, luxuriously furnished with cushioned divans; low antique tables scattered about. There was a thick white carpet on the floor and jade jars and bowls on the tables. The faint perfume was stronger in here. The walls were bare except for a few Chinese scenes in light frames. The brushwork was exquisite and I bent forward, trying to make out the ideograms on the nearest. My guide smiled, his handsome features suffused with pleasure.

"I see you appreciate Chinese art, Mr Faraday. Needless to say, these are originals."

"Very nice indeed," I said, withdrawing my glance from the sea-scape with little sail-boats dotted about.

"If you will wait here, I will announce your presence."

The man in the white suit looked at me with genuine anxiety.

"If I might venture further on your patience, I would strongly advise you to be here when I return."

I looked at him evenly.

"You can rely on it," I said.

He smiled thinly and went up to a door at the far end of the room, knocking at it deferentially before entering. I was left alone for about five minutes. I got out my package of cigarettes and killed the time.

The man in the white suit came back. He looked at me with satisfaction.

"He will see you now, Mr Faraday."

He stood aside and followed me in as I went through the door. It was quite a small room with a big desk up at one end. I didn't have much time for the decor. A tiny Chinese, dressed in a silk robe was sitting behind the desk. He was so diminutive he looked like a wax doll.

He had snow-white hair and a long silver beard which hung down over his chest. His bright beady eyes were full of humour and he burst into a tittering laugh as I got up to him. I stared at my guide and then back to the little man behind the desk.

"Ho Chi Minh, I presume?" I said.

14

The little man's tittering increased in volume. He waved me into a leather chair in front of his desk while the man in the white suit stood back at a respectful distance.

"Li-Fan said you had a sense of humour, Mr Faraday. He has not exaggerated."

"Let's hope we'll have a really hilarious evening together," I said. "What do I call you?"

"Wong will do as well as any other name," said the little man, his eyes still gleaming with good humour.

"That's about as plausible as Ho Chi," I said.

The little man bowed slightly.

"Names are of so little importance," he said smoothly. "You will take some tea with us?"

"Be glad to," I said.

Wong's face was more serious now,

though the humour lingered in the eyes.

"Li-Fan also said you were a sensible man. As always, he has not misrepresented the situation."

"Let's get down to business," I said.

Wong held up his hand.

"You are my guest. There are certain social niceties to be observed."

He pressed a button on his desk. At a sign from him Li-Fan went and fetched another chair and seated himself at the far corner of the desk. So completely had he effaced himself that the focus was entirely on the little man now.

"Like sending your hatchet-man to rough me up," I said.

Mr Wong looked pained. He held up his hands.

"Oh come, sir. This is the twentieth century. We do not do business like that."

"Somebody does," I said, fingering my jaw.

Mr Wong shook his head, an expression of regret in his eyes.

"Violence is old-fashioned and stupid. I am a businessman with a very efficient organization. We do not threaten. And we do not bungle."

"I have been trying to convince Mr Faraday of that," said Li-Fan.

"Well, well, I leave that thought with you, Mr Faraday," said Wong as the far door opened. "We will discuss it again after we have partaken of tea."

A tall Chinese pushed a trolley up to the desk. He wheeled it round to the other side, to Mr Wong's left elbow. With his white, gold-braided jacket and dark trousers he looked like some efficient club-servant out East in an old Somerset Maugham film. He poured expertly, making no sound.

He brought the fragile porcelain bowl and saucer over to me, put down on my side of the desk a dish containing biscuits and little sweet cakes. The fragrance of the tea seemed to fill the room. I sipped appreciatively. Wong watched me with twinkling eyes.

"Good?"

"Very good indeed," I said.

Mr Wong smiled.

"I see you appreciate first-rate things, Mr Faraday."

I shrugged.

"It helps one to get through life."

Mr Wong delicately broke a small biscuit in half and conveyed a fragment to his mouth. Li-Fan kept a solicitous eye on the old man as though to anticipate his every need. There was silence for a minute or so as the almost ritualistic ceremony of the tea-tasting went on.

I hadn't been exaggerating. Like I said it was very good indeed. Presently Wong wiped his hands delicately on a square of lace-edged linen he replaced in his lap. He leaned forward and looked at me with eyes as bright as buttons.

"Now, Mr Faraday, if you have concluded we will get to business."

"Before we start," I said. "I'd just like to straighten something out. About this situation, I mean."

A fleeting expression of impatience crossed Mr Wong's face. He folded his arms carefully across his chest.

"I am not sure I understand you, Mr Faraday."

I smiled.

"I think you understand right enough,

Mr Wong. A character tried to kill me a short while ago. Rightly or wrongly, I put him down as an Oriental. Now you have me brought here . . . "

The old man put up his arm to stop me. His eyes were not smiling now.

"And you thought we had something to do with that, Mr Faraday? You pain me, you really do. I am a businessman. All violence is abhorrent to me. It is true, my business is concerned with the late Dr Hugo Greenbach."

There was a sudden silence in the room.

"You admit you knew him, then?" I said.

The old man shrugged.

"Why should I deny it? But there are always enemies waiting to profit from the inventive mind of such a brilliant man. As I said my organization is interested in him. But we would have protected him, not slaughtered him. That was a dreadful business."

Mr Wong smiled again.

"But you know, of course. You were there, were you not?"

"You seem to know a good deal about my movements, Mr Wong," I said.

"It is my business to know things, Mr Faraday. It is my great regret that I was unable to prevent Dr Greenbach's death. I can assure you it will not go unpunished."

I stared at the man behind the desk for a long moment.

"Just what was this invention? I heard something about a new gasoline method."

Wong shook his head.

"Gasoline, electronics, the thing itself does not matter, Mr Faraday. We are talking about a principle. I am asking you to believe that I had nothing to do with Dr Greenbach's death or the wounding of his assistant, much less the attack on you last night."

I fingered my jaw reflectively.

"You know something about it, anyway."

Li-Fan smiled and stirred in his chair.

"Naturally," he said. "It is a big organization. We were keeping the doctor under observation. We know you had the briefcase. I found you on the floor of the hall last night. That was why your assailants left in a hurry."

He smiled thinly.

"You possibly owe your life to me. Those men would do anything to get what was in that briefcase."

"If the first fact you mentioned is right I'm extremely grateful to you," I said. "But I'm a little dubious about the second statement. How would you know they didn't get what they came for?"

Li-Fan shook his head.

"Because they stayed behind. They were trying to bring you round. One of them was preparing to start operations on you."

I gave him a long, hard look.

"Operations?"

Li-Fan nodded.

"We Chinese are extremely refined at torture, Mr Faraday. As the oldest civilization we early learned the dimensions of pain."

He smiled. I remembered then the man with the gas pistol in the grounds of Greenbach's house and believed him.

"I'll buy it, Mr Wong," I said, turning

back to the old man. "Just what's going on? And how do you think I can help?"

Wong wagged his head a few times, as though to himself.

"You can help, Mr Faraday," he said. "Just listen."

* * *

The blue smoke from my cigarette went up in a slow, wavering stream toward the ceiling.

"You want the formula, then?"

Mr Wong spread his hands wide on the desk.

"Of course, Mr Faraday. It is as simple as that. You might say that Dr Greenbach was encroaching on one of our interests. We tried to buy him out."

Some daylight was coming in now.

"You never at any time threatened him?"

Li-Fan emphatically shook his head.

"I thought I made that amply clear, Mr Faraday."

"Then it must have been the other group," I said. "Just who are they?"

The twinkling humour was back in Mr Wong's eyes now. The Ho Chi Minh beard waggled.

"My nephew was always extremely crude and unreliable."

I stared at him.

"Your nephew?"

I glanced at Li-Fan and then back to the desk again.

"What is this? A tong war? Or a falling out between Triad groups?"

The old man's smile opened wider.

"You deal in very crude generalities, Mr Faraday. The Western mind sees things in such simple terms; a black and white outline instead of infinitely graded segments of grey. Let us just say my nephew and I do not see things in the same light."

"All right," I said. "You're both interested in some process Greenbach's stumbled on. Your group is subtle; your nephew's more crude. Where do I come in?"

Mr Wong spread his hands wide, his expression suddenly shrewd.

"Would ten thousand dollars to begin

with interest you? Plus another twenty thousand when the project is brought to a successful conclusion?"

"It interests me all right," I said. "But just what do you expect?"

Li-Fan leaned forward in his chair.

"You are a very bright and durable man," he said. "We know something of your record. I do not know how you did it but in short I surmise that somewhere between Greenbach's house and your office you disposed of the contents of the briefcase."

Mr Wong's smile broadened while I swapped steady glances with Li-Fan.

"It's a bit far-fetched," I said. "I had time for only a quick glimpse inside the case when I got inside my building. There were a lot of documents in there. Presumably Mr Wong's nephew has them now."

Li-Fan looked serious.

"I hesitate to use a stronger term, Mr Faraday, but I do not believe you. You may not know the value of what you have but you have it just the same."

"Ten thousand dollars, Mr Faraday,"

the old man said softly.

"It's a lot of money," I said.

I shook my head as Wong reached out for a drawer in his desk.

"I'd like some time to think it over," I said.

Mr Wong's expression was regretful.

"Don't take too long, Mr Faraday. We Chinese are extremely patient but we have already run into our reserves over my nephew."

"Give me forty-eight hours," I said. "I may come up with something before then."

Mr Wong beamed.

"Let us hope so."

He put the sheaf of notes back in the drawer again.

"How do I get in touch?" I said.

Li-Fan got up from his chair, bowed ironically.

"We'll be in touch with you," he said.

He put the blindfold over my eyes again and led me out.

15

Li-Fan slid the Buick expertly over to the kerb and cut the motor.

"This will do nicely, Mr Faraday," he said.

He removed the silk scarf from my eyes. I blinked. Neon signs shone through the dusk. I recognized the location. We were about half an hour's drive from the centre of town.

"How will you get back?" I said.

Li-Fan's bronzed features creased into a pleasant smile.

"I shall have no difficulty, Mr Faraday," he said, putting the scarf into a pocket of his jacket. There was a faint squeal of brakes. In the rear mirror I saw the blue Studebaker pull up a dozen yards behind us. Li-Fan showed no sign of moving so I lit a cigarette. I put the spent match-stalk in the dashboard tray and offered him the pack. He shook his head.

"I don't indulge. I regard all such

habits as a form of weakness."

He turned toward me in the driving-seat.

"Have you given further thought to Mr Wong's suggestion?"

I feathered out blue smoke, watching the jagged edges of a red neon sign making misty patterns through the darkness of the windshield.

"I've thought about it plenty," I said.

Li-Fan gave his teeth another brief airing.

"It is a great deal of money, is it not?"

"I thought about the money," I said. "I also thought about the situation."

Li-Fan shifted in his seat. His face wore an infinitely patient expression.

"You mean the risk?"

"Partly," I said.

Li-Fan's eyes were bland and expressionless.

"You are no stranger to risk, Mr Faraday. Think what you could do with the money."

"I can't spend it if I'm dead," I said.

Li-Fan looked pained.

"Who said anything about being dead?" he said.

I shook my head.

"You misunderstand me, Li-Fan. I'm talking about Mr Wong's nephew's mob. They don't seem to operate with your finesse."

Li-Fan picked an invisible piece of lint off the lapel of his immaculate suit and held it up for inspection against the faint glow of the distant neon.

"You can trust us to keep them off your neck, Mr Faraday."

"Like you did last night?" I said.

Li-Fan shook his head.

"You were not working for us, then, Mr Faraday."

"Makes a difference, does it?"

"Believe me, it makes a great deal of difference, Mr Faraday."

I gave him a long, hard stare.

"Well, maybe," I said. "If Mr Wong is the top man you'll be Red-Stick, if I know anything of the Triads."

Li-Fan chuckled.

"You will insist on melodrama, Mr Faraday."

172

"If I do it's probably under the influence of the Chinese Theatre," I told him.

Li-Fan made an elegant twirling motion with his fingers, presumably to get rid of the lint.

"Assuming you are right and adopting your own crude and over-simplified terms, do I look like an enforcer? Moreover, do I behave like one?"

"That's what's got me guessing," I said.

Li-Fan slid out the driving seat with a swift, supple movement and I got behind the wheel. He held out his hand. To my surprise I found myself taking it.

"Just one last word of advice, Mr Faraday. I have come to like you in the short time I have known you. Basically, you are my kind of person. Please accept Mr Wong's offer. And don't take too long about it. Good night."

He smiled pleasantly again and melted back into the shadows. A moment later the motor of the Studebaker gunned up, the main beams flicked on and it crunched out from the kerb, made a

U-turn and dissolved back into the dusk again. I sat and finished my cigarette, chewing over the events of the evening. I looked at my wrist-watch. It was already eight. I'd get outside some food before I made my next move. I started the motor and drove back into town.

★ ★ ★

Dillon lived in a chintzy apartment block in a modern courtyard development, complete with ornamental fountains, communal swimpool, centrally heated garages and concierge service. It was just turned half-nine when I got there and I was prepared to find him out. But he showed at the first buzz of the bell. His usually immaculate persona looked considerably dented and his face almost haggard in the dim corridor lighting. His eyes showed surprise and then he had recovered himself.

"I've been trying to get you all day," he snapped.

"You started pretty late," I said. "I was there until mid-afternoon."

He scowled but said nothing. He unlatched the chain from the door.

"You'd better come in," he said grudgingly.

He wore a scarlet silk dressing gown over his cream silk shirt and dark trousers.

"It's time for some plain talking," I said.

Now that I was in the room Dillon looked yellow. His usually immaculate style had been completely shattered. He waved a hand helplessly toward a leather divan. I sat down and watched while he fussed around an ornate cocktail cabinet.

"I could use a whisky," I said. "Water and ice."

Dillon mixed the drinks with a trembling hand. He came over toward me and handed me the glass.

"God, this is a mess," he said tonelessly.

He sat down at the other end of the divan and looked at me with listless eyes.

"If only you hadn't been off last night," he said.

"It's no good talking about that now,"

I said. "We've got other things to think about. I was at the house last night. I was just too late. Someone was already inside."

Dillon's jaw dropped. He stared at me incredulously.

"You know what you're saying, Faraday?"

"Sure I know," I told him. "We're both in this up to our necks. That's why we've got to get at the facts."

Dillon gulped and swallowed the contents of his glass. Some of the colour was coming back to his cheeks. I looked round the shadowy apartment. The light was coming from two standard lamps. The decor was Spanish hacienda style; rough white walls hung with oils in gold frames; iron grille-work; plenty of leather upholstered furniture. I stared at Dillon thoughtfully.

"As a lawyer," he said slowly, "there's a good deal I could say about the situation. As a citizen my first instinct is to go to the police."

"As a private eye, I agree with you," I said. "But there's a lot of good reasons against. And as a private citizen as well as a licensed dick I have a personal objection to getting my butt shot off."

Dillon looked at me over the rim of his empty glass.

"I'm not quite sure I understand what you mean, Faraday."

I shook my head.

"You know what I mean all right. Greenbach was working on something big. Right? Something big enough for the mobs to be interested in."

Dillon half-got up from the divan, thought better of it.

"Don't waste your breath," I told him. "Something to do with gasoline, wasn't it."

Little red spots were burning on Dillon's cheeks.

"How you came to know that . . . " he began.

"Never mind how," I said. "I do know and I think it's time we had some frankness between us. If I'm to help you, that is."

Dillon stared at me with something of his old manner.

177

"I don't like your tone, Faraday," he blustered.

"I don't like your case," I said. "But I'm going on with it. I've been beaten up, gassed, threatened and shot at so far. I could have been dead half a dozen times but for luck and my own wits. Now I want to see you come up with something."

The lawyer's face was green now. He made a convulsive effort to get a grip on his nerves. He put out his hand in a placatory gesture.

"I'm sorry, Mr Faraday," he said finally. "I know I have an unfortunate manner sometimes. I'm not ungrateful for what you've done. Believe me, I'm shocked both at what you've just told me and at Greenbach's death. And it's true I've been less than frank with you. It's time to lay my cards on the table."

I held out my empty glass.

"All right," I said. "No hard feelings. And you can re-fill that at the same time you're laying your cards out."

He took the glass with a wry smile and went over to the cocktail cabinet.

I glanced round the apartment again. There was a woman's white fox-fur stole lying on a chair near a mahogany door up a flight of shallow wooden steps at one side of the big room. Dillon must have been watching me in the mirror.

"The lady prefers discretion, Mr Faraday. I'm sure you understand."

I grinned.

"I'm as understanding as the next man about things like that. Normally I wouldn't have disturbed you except for emergency. And this looks like being a major emergency."

Dillon frowned. For the moment the sharp, well-groomed look had gone. His grey eyes were worried and even his expensive haircut seemed rumpled. He sat on an arm of the divan, up at the other end and looked at me without speaking. I raised my glass in an ironic salute. He leaned forward, moodily swilling the contents of his tumbler.

"As I said, Faraday, I haven't been entirely frank with you," he said softly. "Dr Greenbach, as you know, was a brilliant chemist. Both at Arnos

Chemicals and outside he has been working on gasoline products, with sometimes startling results. I had a part interest in his private research and had invested some money in his experiments."

"It would have helped if you'd come out into the open sooner," I said.

Dillon shook his head.

"Greenbach had impressed upon me absolute discretion in the matter," he said. "I had to string along with him. How you got on to this I don't know . . . "

"The same way as other people," I said. "You told me he'd been threatened. What you didn't tell me was that the Triads were involved."

Dillon's complexion didn't exactly turn green but he was very close to it. His lower jaw sagged and he suddenly looked a lot older than his years.

"The Triads? The Chinese secret societies?"

"You didn't know that?" I said.

Dillon shook his head, his lips trembling.

"Greenbach was a very secretive character. He told me he'd been visited once at his home by a man representing a group of people who wanted part of the operation. Later, he was threatened by letter."

"You didn't see this letter?"

Dillon shook his head.

"Greenbach said he burned it. He was an extraordinary man. Fear didn't exist in his vocabulary."

"It didn't get him very far," I said. "Someone lost patience with him. It was unfortunate for the girl secretary too."

Dillon looked uncomfortable.

"I did not realize this would happen, Mr Faraday. She will be taken care of."

"If she lives," I said.

"If she lives," Dillon repeated softly. "The bulletins earlier today said she had a good chance of recovery."

"Just see that you do take care of her," I said. "There have been the attempts to kill me. Not to mention the Chinese lifting a briefcase Greenbach was carrying."

Dillon lifted up his hand.

"I swear I did not know things would become so dangerous, Mr Faraday. But the Triads? What can we do?"

"Very little," I said. "They're a big organization. But I've got a tame one nibbling at my fingers at the moment. I'd like a crack at the people who killed Greenbach. So I'm playing along. Which is why I don't want you to put a foot wrong."

"How could I do that?" said Dillon quickly.

"By withholding information for one thing," I said levelly. "Just keep your mouth shut. No police, no nothing. And if you think of anything else that might help I'm in the book."

"By all means, Mr Faraday," said Dillon absently. "You will not find me ungrateful."

I finished off my drink.

"I'm banking on it," I told him.

He didn't say anything else. I went on out and left him sitting there in the twilight of the shaded lamps, staring at something I couldn't see, like he was face to face with reality for the first time in his life.

16

It was around ten-thirty when I reached Zelda van Opper's apartment building. A thin rain had been falling again and the streets were slick and shining under the harsh light of the street-lamps. I pulled the Buick into a layby carved out of solid rock outside the Schuyler Apartments.

There were a number of other cars already there and I looked carefully to make sure they were all empty. You're getting to be a regular old maid, Faraday, I told myself. Guess my nerves were still a little frayed. I was beginning to see Chinese behind every bush. Which wasn't very difficult in L.A.

I got out the Buick and slammed the door. The air was fresh and clean-smelling after the rain and the perfume of flowers came from off the top of the bank where shaved lawns stretched away to the ornamental foliage in rear. There were big oaks in the grounds and they cast heavy shadows in the floodlighting as I walked up the pink tarmac driveway into the court of the apartments.

The white façade of the building was flood-lit too and the name of the apartments, spelled out in silver-chrome lettering on the entrance canopy, winked in the light. Above, the bulk of the building was lost in the purple dusk of the night sky. There were ornamental rose-bushes set about in yellow tubs on the terrazzo tiling and the brass-fitted swing doors had been freshly burnished. It was a nice set-up and I guessed the van Opper number must have been highly paid to have afforded to live here.

But then secretaries got paid the earth these days. You're in the wrong profession, Mike, I told myself. I grinned. Wrong sex too, come to that. I couldn't see myself earning that sort of money, even as a male secretary. I rode with the joke which lasted me all the way through the lobby. I looked up the girl's apartment number on a board in the vestibule and buttoned my way up to the twelfth floor in a steel and teak cage.

There didn't seem to be any people around this time of the evening and the whole building had a sort of discreet calm about it that comes with money and the good organization and service the money brings. I got out at the twelfth and padded my way along the thickly carpeted corridor. I was a little wary. I guessed the police would have gone over the girl's apartment and I was hoping they wouldn't still be around.

I hadn't seen any sign of unusual activity when I came in and there was certainly no guard on the girl's door. I decided to play it the discreet way. If they had a guard inside I'd ask for some fictitious character and make like I'd gotten the wrong floor. As I moved down the corridor the papers I carried in my billfold seemed to be burning a hole through my suit. I hadn't been able to figure them out yet but I was certain they represented something important.

Maybe Zelda van Opper would have known. Or at any rate there might be more documentation in her apartment which might throw light on the problem.

It was obvious that sometimes she would take material from Greenbach home. Leastways, I hoped so. That was why I was here. At the moment I was like a man moving through the darkness with a blindfold on. With the blindfold off I'd still be handicapped. I stopped beating my brains out and got up to the door of Apartment 49.

I stood listening to the pumping of my heart and the faint hum of the air-conditioning and for perhaps the thousandth time breathed in the faint perfume that these places always spread about the corridors. It was some thing that went with money and status and an ordered life-style. Something that I'd likely never have. I gave up the Ella Wheeler Wilcox reminiscing and hit the button.

I stood and listened to its faint buzz reverberating from the interior. I put my ear close to the panel. There was no sound from within. Nothing except the dead, empty atmosphere that's unmistakable. I couldn't explain it. It was something that came with the job and stemmed from years of such fruitless expeditions. I sighed and hit the button again. Then I tried the handle. The door opened easily to my touch.

I slid through into darkness. I stood in the semi-gloom of the apartment and waited for my eyes to adjust to the subdued light. There was the reflected glow of neon coming in from the horizon and the blurred outlines of furniture started swimming into vision as a negative is developed in a photographic dish.

I went over to the big French windows. The drapes were half-pulled across and I slid them all the way over. Then I padded toward a standard lamp I'd noticed in one corner and switched it on. The warm glow it made showed me unmistakable signs of police presence. Pictures were hanging slightly crooked, ornaments and items had been moved on desk tops and a few drawers in a handsome walnut bureau near the lamp had been left almost closed but not quite.

I sighed. It didn't look as though I'd be left with much. But one never knew. I went through the drawers of the bureau.

I didn't know what I was looking for but I'd recognize it when I saw it. It was quiet in here, apart from the faint hum of the air-conditioning and I figured I'd be able to hear if anyone came along the corridor. The unlocked door worried me a little. I went over and snubbed and buttoned it into the locked position.

Maybe the police had left it unlocked. Or more likely the management of the apartments meant to go over it as the owner would obviously be in hospital for some time. I wandered back into the middle of the room and stared round slowly, hoping for some sign. I didn't get any bright ideas like that. I risked a cigarette, put the spent match-stalk back in the box. There was the stale smell of cigar-smoke in the air anyway which overlaid my smoke. The place reeked of the heavy hand of the official force.

I walked back over toward the desk again. I stood by the window and stared at the drawers and the slightly disarranged articles. Some of them were heavy and the slight impressions they'd made on the wood of the table-tops and desk showed clearly where they'd been shifted. Didn't seem possible there would be anything left for me.

I blew out a thin plume of smoke and eyed the cabinet photograph of the van Opper girl which stood on the grey leather surface of the desk. That's when the velvet drapes at my back billowed and something as big and heavy as a beer-truck drove all the breath out of me. I went forward and down with a crash that shook the building.

* * *

I wriggled aside, reaching for the Smith-Wesson. A hand like steel came through the drapes, clamped my wrist. I was winded but my reflexes were working fine now. I clubbed my left and struck through the drapes. My fist connected with flesh and there was a grunt but the grip on my wrist hardly relaxed. I stopped trying for the Smith-Wesson then and dived forward.

I almost broke the wrist-hold but the

big man who was leeching on to me was pretty durable. He stopped trying too and came with me. I half-dragged him clear of the curtains. He was a smart-looking young man dressed in an immaculate lightweight grey suit and with tousled blond hair. He had a clean-cut look that some pilots and army officers have. His blue eyes glared at me and he clung desperately to my wrist while he flailed ineffectually in my direction with his right hand and arm, which was twisted up behind him.

I pulled forward more, on to the carpet, effectively neutralizing his blows. We both stayed like that for a few seconds, panting. I looked at him calmly.

"This is pretty futile," I said. "Won't you introduce yourself?"

"Go fry an egg," he said aggressively. I grinned.

"My name's Faraday," I said. "I'm a private investigator working on a case."

He increased his grip, perspiration running down into his eyes.

"What are you doing in Zelda's room, then?"

"Same thing as you," I told him. "Snooping."

He blinked and his grip relaxed a little.

"I have a perfect right to be here."

"Ah, there you have me," I said. "But if it's any use to you I was trying to pick up a lead on the men who killed her boss and wounded her."

The young man bared his teeth sardonically.

"I don't buy it, Faraday."

"I'm not selling anything," I said. "But if you don't believe me, you'll find a billfold in my breast-pocket. It contains a photostat of my licence which will identify me."

He thought about this for a minute, varied emotions flitting across his face. I eased my own grip and his right hand cautiously came forward, rummaged in my pocket, came up with the billfold.

"The leather wallet just inside the flap," I said.

He flipped it open, keeping his eyes on my face. He glanced downward, taking in the details.

"Looks genuine," he grudgingly admitted. "Guess we ought to get up. But no funny business."

"Sure," I said. "You attacked me, remember. You haven't introduced yourself yet."

He let go my wrist, looking at me warily. We both got up awkwardly, dusting ourselves down. I went over and sat on the edge of the desk and stared at him.

"My name's Quincey Anderson," he said. "Zelda and I were going to get married."

"You still are," I said. "Last I heard she was doing fine."

A light came into his eyes, stayed there before he lowered his gaze.

"You haven't cleared yourself yet, Mr Faraday," he said. "And you've no right here at all."

"I plead guilty to the second charge," I said. "I don't have to clear myself with anyone. I was in the room a few seconds after Greenbach and Miss van Opper got shot. I was too late to help. I don't want to be immodest but if your fiancée's pulling through it's because I treated her wound and called the ambulance."

Anderson looked at me, his jaw clenched; his mouth opened once or twice but no sound came out for several seconds.

"I'd like to believe that, Mr Faraday. I'd always be in your debt."

"I don't give a damn whether you do or not," I said. "I've only told you because I think you're on the up and up."

He nodded absently. He sat down hesitantly on a divan a few yards away from me.

"I don't know what to make of this," he said. "Zelda gave me the key of her apartment. I had a lot of trouble with the police this morning."

"I'll bet," I said.

"I'd forgotten to lock the door when they left," he said. "I felt so miserable I just hung around. They wouldn't let me see her at the hospital. Then I heard the buzzer go and I decided to hide and find out what happened."

I looked at him sharply.

"That sounds suspicious in itself," I said.

He shook his head.

"Maybe. But there was a phone-call earlier today. A man with a foreign voice. It warned me I'd get the same as Zelda if I tried to mess in his affairs."

I rubbed my chin and put my billfold away.

"Interesting," I said. "You told the police?"

He nodded.

"They were interested all right but my guess is they haven't any idea what's going on."

"That's right," I said.

Anderson stared at me for perhaps fifteen seconds.

"You mean you haven't told the police anything about the shoot-out? That you were there?"

I shook my head.

"I couldn't afford to. Not at this stage. And I don't want you to say anything either."

He shut his mouth in a thin, firm line;

his eyes still looked suspicious.

"You got any identification?" I said.

He smiled then. He fished around in his pocket.

"Driver's licence. That do?"

He threw it over to me. I studied it. He was Quincey Anderson all right. He had an address in San Francisco.

"What do you do for a living or is it restricted?" I said.

He shook his head.

"I used to be a commercial airline pilot. Now I run my own secretarial agency. Zelda's going to be a partner in the business when we're married."

"Sounds nice," I said. "What do you know about all this?"

He looked at me quickly.

"The shooting? Nothing at all. I only arrived in town a couple of days ago."

I gave him a sympathetic look.

"Looks like we're both in trouble, Mr Anderson. How about pooling our resources. You look — and feel — like a handy man in a roughhouse."

Anderson grinned again. He got up and came over toward me.

"Anything to help Zelda, Mr Faraday. And you can rely on my discretion."

"We'll get along just fine," I said.

He held out his hand for me to shake.

17

I pulled the Buick up at an amber light and sat frowning thoughtfully at the neon-slashed darkness in front of the windshield. Anderson was quiet at my side, his strong, durable face outwardly relaxed. He'd rung the hospital just before we left the apartment. The van Opper girl was out of danger. Leastways, you've done some good in this world, Faraday, I told myself.

I put the heap in gear and drew away from the lights, turning off up into the hills where I'd followed Greenbach. It seemed like years ago now. It was a long shot, but it was all I had to make some sense out of the muddle.

"You know what we're doing tonight's illegal?" I said.

Anderson grinned.

"Sure," he said cheerfully. "Most worthwhile things are."

I looked at him sharply.

"There could be danger."

"I can take care of myself," he said. "Besides, you have a gun, haven't you?"

I shrugged.

"You have touching faith in my abilities."

There was a warm glint in Anderson's eyes. He shook his head.

"You saved Zelda, Mr Faraday. I owe you a good deal. My future even. I'd follow you to hell if necessary."

"I hope it won't be that far," I said.

Quincey Anderson grinned again.

"Besides, I've got a lot of natural curiosity. I want to see just what it is that Zelda got involved in. It had to be something extraordinary for these people to go to such lengths."

"Just my opinion," I said.

I drifted into an S-bend, dust rising beneath the wheels in the moonlight.

"You don't go for the gasoline angle?" Quincey Anderson said.

I shook my head.

"It's possible but the Chinese don't bother with that sort of stuff. Gasoline products need a hell of a lot of knowhow; corporations, crooked lawyers and syndicates. But not the Triads."

Anderson looked curiously at the black metal box with the heavy duty flex that sat on the front bench seat between us.

"You think this is the answer?"

"It may be," I said. "Why the hell should Greenbach and your girl-friend sit up there switching TV programmes around?"

A little hardness was back in Anderson's eyes.

"I told you Zelda had nothing to do with this, Mr Faraday. That still stands."

"No-one ever said she did," I told him. "But she typed all these figures and formulae on the papers I have in my pocket. Most of the secretaries who deal with this material don't know what the hell it means."

Anderson relaxed in his seat again.

"Sure, Mr Faraday. It's just that I see red when I think of Zelda."

"Keep on seeing red," I said. "Only reserve it for the opposition."

We were going up the last mile

of roadway now. The Buick suddenly seemed very exposed in the moonlight.

"What's the drill?" Anderson said as I drifted the automobile over the last few hundred yards before turning off into the shadows of overhanging trees on the verge.

"We just break in," I said. "It's a minor offence compared to the things I got hanging over me."

Anderson nodded, a strange look on his face.

"Pretty interesting ride," he said.

I killed the motor and looked back down the road. Nothing moved in all the vast expanse of moonlight. But I had an uneasy sixth sense tonight. It was something that had stayed with me all the time I went back to the office and dug Greenbach's gimmick out of the sand of the firebucket. I could have sworn we weren't followed yet I remembered Li-Fan and Mr Wong and the power they wielded and I felt uncomfortable around my neck muscles.

That was an infallible sign with me that something was wrong. So I put my keys in my pocket and broke out the Smith-Wesson, throwing off the safety. I remembered too the muscle merchant with the gas pistol. I aimed to throw lead first if trouble broke. We got out the car and quietly closed the doors.

"You'd better stay here," I said.

Anderson shook his head, flexing his heavy shoulder muscles.

"Not a chance, Mr Faraday. I said I was in. I mean all the way."

I gave him a long, hard look.

"All right," I said. "But just remember you're unarmed. Stick close and take your cues from me."

Anderson grinned, his teeth glinting in the moonlight.

"Sure, Mr Faraday. Anything you say."

The big, Spanish-style mansion looked dead and bereft like its owner. We walked up the dusty path in the moonlight, through the white picket fences of the entrance and along the pink-floored driveway. Like before I skirted the terrace and the swim-pool area and led the way past the four-car garage and the stable block. The perfume of the jacarandas was like an aching nerve in the gum after a tooth had long been pulled.

Anderson drew up his brows and frowned at the spread.

"Just what Zelda told me, Mr Faraday."

"Like what?" I said, shooting quick glances around me as I walked. But nothing moved in the moonlight except the tops of the trees in the warm breeze.

"Too much money for an industrial chemist."

I nodded.

"The young lady sounds very shrewd as well as being extremely ornamental."

"She is," Anderson said.

"So why should she act like she was the worse for drink when she was with Greenbach?" I said.

We were going round the side of the house now, in the shadows, making for the rear. Anderson stopped near the big iron gate.

"You saw her?"

"Sure," I said. "It was up at Garibaldi's one night. I thought she was Greenbach's girl-friend. She looked like she was

202

pickled to the gills. But once she got up here she was absolutely sober."

Anderson nodded thoughtfully.

"I didn't like that part of it," he said. "It was camouflage. It happened a few times when he had to meet Zelda in public places. She's a looker, as you know. It suited him to have people think there was something personal in their relationship. But it was a mask for his business activities. And he paid Zelda well for the act."

"She told you about it, then?"

He nodded again. We were going through the rear garden now, past the sunken pool and on to the terrace. I stopped in front of the picture windows of the room where Greenbach and the girl had been.

"She was a hundred per cent straight, Mr Faraday," Anderson said.

"You're like me," I said. "You think he had something to hide? Other than gasoline formulae or business interests?"

Anderson stood teetering on his heels, his honest, open face clouded in the moonlight.

"I didn't even know the man, Mr Faraday. But from what Zelda let drop from time to time I figured him for some kind of high class crook."

I stared at him for a long moment.

"It took me a while but I'd been coming to the same conclusion myself," I said. "Let's get at it."

I picked up a rock from the border at the edge of the terrace and smashed the picture window in.

★ ★ ★

Anderson stared at the sheet of figures, his face blank. We had the drapes across the window and a small light on up near the TV set. It seemed like years since the van Opper girl and Greenbach sat here, with him switching the programmes like his life depended on it. Maybe it had at that.

"Any ideas?" I said.

He shook his head.

"A few, maybe. Nothing to do with gasoline, of course."

"Like I figured," I told him.

We sat at the table, with him diagonally across from me. He squinted at the sheets.

"I took a course in chemistry once. Flunked it, naturally. This looks more like drugs."

I smiled slowly.

"The Triad operations are all concerned with drugs, protection and allied rackets. I'm glad to have my hunch strengthened."

I smoked in silence for a moment or two. Anderson glanced across at the television set in the corner. Like I said it was a big cabinet model half-slewed away from the window.

"You want to try and see how this gadget works?"

"That's what we're here for, isn't it?"

I got up and walked over toward it. It was already plugged in to a heavy duty socket in the room skirting board and I flipped the toggle switch on with my foot. I studied the controls. They looked unusually complicated.

Anderson got up and came over to join me. He looked at the black switch unit I'd picked up from the table.

"There's usually a special socket at the back for these. It's a four-pin."

I nodded. I moved over and walked round in back of the big set. There were a number of sockets there not doing anything but only one with four pins. The set was switched on now, giving out an audible hum but there was only a blank blue screen. Anderson put out his hand to the station button but I stopped him.

"Let's leave it like it is, shall we?"

He shrugged, his face blank and expressionless.

"Will it be any good on a blank channel?"

"That's what I want to find out," I said.

I plugged the black box mechanism into the socket in rear of the set. Nothing happened. I stood looking at the machine for a long minute. The signal strength was about right now. I punched the programme button. The close-up of three heavies filled the screen. We were right in the middle of a Grade-B Western. Fortunately the sound was switched off.

I shifted channels again, looked silently at the shimmering blue particles of the dead screen.

"The set's working all right," Anderson said.

I nodded.

"So we got to see what this gadget does."

There was a small red button at one side of the console I noticed as I checked the mechanism. I punched it. There was an exclamation from Anderson. I looked up. The screen was filled with a mass of shimmering bluish figures and letters.

"Looks like we got something," he said.

"Maybe," I told him.

I stared at the figures thoughtfully. Then I went over toward the window. From there the screen and its images was invisible, just like the night I was outside. I looked at Anderson, all sorts of ratchets clicking around in my mind. Trouble is they weren't engaging with anything. I had an idea then.

"Sit down in that chair," I told him.

He stared at me for a moment and then did as I said.

"Now try the red knob."

He punched it again.

"The figures have changed," he said.

There was a note of excitement in his voice which hadn't been there before.

"Keep on going," I told him.

Anderson put a new set of figures on the screen. I could tell that because of the changes in the shimmering reflections from the set which passed across his face. I felt something growing inside me; something which had been absent throughout the case. Anderson turned round, examining my features.

"What is it?" he said like he could see what I was thinking.

"Daylight at last," I said.

I went back over to him, sat down at the table next him and stared at the new set of figures on the screen.

"Lone Ranger, hell!" I said.

Anderson smiled politely.

"Apart from the fact that I don't know what the devil you're talking about, Mr Faraday, I'd say you were on to something."

I grinned.

"Maybe," I said. "Maybe not. I was just thinking about Stella."

I stared moodily at the screen again.

"Leastways, I know what Greenbach and your fiancée were doing that night. Now, if we understood what the figures meant . . ."

Anderson looked at me quickly.

"I don't get you," he said.

"Let's slice it another way," I said. "You hit the button first time off. Let's say it's drugs. Now we got a code. Could there be some way to transmit this material?"

Anderson stared at me for a long moment.

"Sure," he said. "I read something in an electronics magazine."

"Some gasoline substitute," I said. "Greenbach was transmitting instructions to a drugs ring."

18

There was a long silence between us. I looked at the bluish figures on the screen. Then I hit the main button and the image disappeared.

"How would they work it?" I said. "There are laws about transmissions and frequencies and things like that."

Anderson looked at me stonily.

"There are ways," he said. "If Greenbach was clever enough."

"He was clever enough," I said. "Like what?"

Anderson shrugged. He drew his chair closer to me at the table, his frank, open face furrowed.

"This won't reflect on Zelda, will it?"

"I don't get you," I said.

Anderson shrugged again. He contrived to make the gesture look worried too.

"I mean if Greenbach was mixed up in a racket."

I shook my head.

"Not if she didn't know what she was doing. And she didn't know, did she? Not after what you told me coming in."

Anderson licked his lips. Strain was showing in back of his eyes.

"I'd stake my life on it, Mr Faraday. Zelda didn't know anything about this. She was just acting as a temporary secretary for the doctor."

"She's in the clear, then," I said.

I sat staring at the blank screen, my ratchets still working overtime. The wind made creaking noises at the corner of the building. Far away, on the road in the middle distance, the rumble of a heavy truck came up to us as a low vibration, fretted into segments by the wind.

"How would they work it?" I said. "According to your magazine on electronics?"

Anderson shot me an apologetic look.

"I'm no expert," he said.

"Just draw me a simple picture based on your reading," I said.

"Well, like I said, Mr Faraday, I have more than a passing interest in electronics

211

and gadgetry. It's something I share with Zelda."

"She said nothing to you about this television business with Greenbach?"

Anderson shook his head.

"She's a confidential secretary, Mr Faraday. It means just that with her. But I do know Greenbach was paying her plenty to keep his affairs under tabs."

I nodded.

"It figures, but I just wondered. Let's get back on to this set-up. How would Greenbach have worked it?"

Anderson fixed me with his frank blue eyes.

"I don't know how he did it, Mr Faraday. It was his field, after all. But I have an idea how it could have been done."

"Let's have it."

Anderson looked at me sombrely in the thick silence of the room.

"This is only stuff I've read, of course. It all boils down to teletext."

"What's that?" I asked.

Anderson grinned crookedly.

"Patience, Mr Faraday."

"It's not my strong point," I told him.

He cleared his throat.

"Well, put simply, it's nothing more than a generic name for a system of transmitting data to TV sets by the use of coded electronic impulses."

"You're interesting me," I said.

"It's only a long shot, Mr Faraday."

"Let's have some more of it," I said.

Anderson shrugged.

"That's it, more or less. The information's carried on the unused lines of your picture. The receiving set has to be equipped with a teletext decoder so that the transmitted data can be displayed on the screen."

I sat back in my chair and set fire to another cigarette. I watched the thin whorls of smoke trickling lazily up to the ceiling.

"So Greenbach would have had to have invented a miniaturized transmitter? By pre-setting it and carrying it around he could have transmitted material to other sets?"

"Put baldly, yes," Anderson said. "If

213

he was clever enough."

"He was clever enough," I said. "And the transmitter is in that black box there. That was what the Chinese were after."

"So what does it all add up to, Mr Faraday?"

"A fool-proof system," I said. "I don't quite know what Greenbach was transmitting but it could have been instructions for distribution of dope."

"With the traffickers sitting watching their TV sets at pre-arranged times and dates?" said Anderson admiringly.

I pulled heavily at my cigarette and looked at him through the smoke.

"Could be," I said.

"In which case we might well be in some danger," Anderson said.

A pistol had somehow grown into his fist. The gun blammed and flame blossomed from the barrel as I threw myself down.

* * *

I hit the floor with a bone-jarring thud and rolled away. Anderson fired again while I was doing that and I heard the window glass in back of me splinter. The shaded light went out as I got to the Smith-Wesson.

"Behind you."

Anderson's voice sounded unsteady.

"What the hell are you playing at?" I said.

Anderson crawled closer.

"I just saved you from being shot. There was someone coming up to the window. I saw him through the gap in the drapes."

"Good thing you told me," I said. "I was just aiming to put a slug between your eyes."

Anderson's voice still sounded worried.

"There was no time to warn you, Mr Faraday."

"Never mind," I said. "You must have scared hell out of somebody. Which makes two of us."

Anderson laughed softly.

"Get over near the door," I told him. "We don't want to be surprised. I'll look after the window. How come you carry a gun?"

"It's something I use when I'm flying," Anderson said. "I'm licensed. And what with the hi-jacking scares I figured it might come in useful."

"Why didn't you tell me?" I said.

"I was waiting until I could trust you," Anderson whispered.

I crawled to the window, raised my head slightly above floor level. There was some moonlight coming in. Enough for my purpose. While I was doing that something shattered the glass and tore a great sliver out the floor about a yard behind me. Fragments of glass and splinters of wood whined about the room. I hit the deck again and stayed there.

"If you've got any ideas I'd like to hear them," I told Anderson.

"You're the professional," he said. "I'll do what has to be done so long as you give the orders."

"Fair enough," I said. "As soon as anything occurs to me I'll let you know."

I couldn't see Anderson's face properly but I sensed rather than saw the grin on his face. It was just an instinct. I knew then I could trust him to carry out his part of the bargain. I crawled away from the window.

A thin, reedy voice like the piping of a wind instrument came to us over the faint breeze which was now rising.

"Mr Faraday, it is useless to resist. You have something we want."

"Why don't you come in and get it?" I shouted back.

There was a long silence. It was brighter in the room now that my eyes had gotten used to the light. The curtains fluttered in the breeze and a sliver of broken glass, dislodged by their restlessness, fell to the floor with a noise like the scratching of a dead man's finger-nail. I grinned to myself. That's a hell of a simile, Mike, even for you.

"Mr Faraday."

The high voice was infinitely patient.

"We could easily do that but what is the point of unnecessary bloodshed. Give us the material we want and we will let you go unharmed."

"Sure," I said. "I learned about that one in my first issue of *The Compleat Detective*."

"How am I doing?" I asked Anderson.

There was a faint edge to his voice but it was steady enough.

"All right so far. If there's anything I disagree with I'll let you know."

"You do that," I said. "In the meantime keep your eyes peeled. The inner door's locked, I take it?"

"Sure," Anderson said. "I saw to that as soon as I got over here."

"We'll make it all right," I said. "Just let every shot count. They'll be in here soon. That little man's patience won't last long."

I crawled farther over, straining my ears. There was no sound of anything outside, other than the faint fretting of wind in the trees and round the corners of the house. The moonlight shone down bland and antiseptic on the shattered window and the faint garden beyond.

"Mr Faraday."

The piping voice was becoming irritable.

"We will give you just five minutes. Then we are coming in."

I looked moodily at the Smith-Wesson, checked the shells in the chambers.

"It's your own risk," I shouted. "You better have your insurance policy up to date."

"What about ringing the police?" Anderson said.

I shook my head.

"Three reasons."

"Such as?"

There was a wealth of resignation in his voice. He was learning fast.

"Wires probably cut," I said. "Secondly, I'd have too much to explain. Thirdly, it would be long over by the time they got out here."

Anderson made a gulping noise. Leastways, it sounded like it.

"You convince me, Mr Faraday. We'll just have to take pot luck."

"I've been in worse spots," I said. "And I was usually alone."

I tried to sound cheerful but somehow I didn't think I was making too good a job of it.

"It's your show, Mr Faraday."

"That's just the rub," I told him. "We got three minutes yet. That's a long time under certain circumstances."

"Like it gives them more opportunity to get in position," Anderson said.

"They were in position long ago," I said. "We're dealing with pros. They were just trying to draw our fire earlier. They won't come in until they're sure they can make it effective."

"How about getting up top?" Anderson said.

"Too late," I said. "My guess is that they're in the house already. The talk is just to keep us occupied. Look after the door. I'll handle the rest."

I glanced at the luminous dial of my watch again. A minute and a half to go.

"You'd better stand by," I told Anderson. "These characters won't give us any further warning."

The last minute crawled away. The second hand of my watch had just clipped the five when something struck the door and sent shards of wood bouncing angrily round the room. Anderson was away from the panel and well into the edge of the wall; his reflexes were pretty good under the circumstances. He pumped one shot through the door, about half-way up.

The muzzle flash lit the room. There was a deadly silence and then something slumped the other side of the door and hit the floor like a wet sack.

"You struck gold," I said. "Just keep it up."

There was a slithering noise beyond the door.

"They're dragging him away," Anderson whispered. "Shall I let go again?"

"Save your ammunition," I said. "They were just testing the defences. They'll be back."

My eyes were used to the light now and I could see the foliage beyond the window and every fold and stitch of material in the curtains. I saw something else too. Something that shouldn't have been there. Something low down, on the edge of the window frame where a big fragment of glass had been torn out. Something big and yellow that looked like a bunch of bananas.

It was a well-worn simile but it was all I could come up with for the moment. Appropriate anyway. What I was looking at was the knuckles belonging to a hand so big that its owner must have been a giant. I saw the frame tremble slightly as the owner of the knuckles tested the pressure. He was trying to ease the window up but it was locked so he didn't have any luck. A faint shadow moved, and the smooth frame at the base of the window took an irregular outline.

Glass and woodwork splintered as the huge man in the stocking-mask launched himself through the window at me. I went over backward as the room blacked out, the blam of the Smith-Wesson seeming to take the top of my head off.

19

The flash from the muzzle appeared to scorch my face, we were working at such close quarters. I heard Anderson's gun crack then and the room was filled with smoke but I had no room for sideshows. My cheeks were stinging and my eyes blinded as I crashed back into a table at the side of the room. The man in the stocking-mask kept on going and I heard glass splinter again. I didn't have time to see whether the sound came from the window or from inside the room.

I rolled over and kept on rolling as two more reports sounded; another shadow passed across the window. I got off a snap-shot. The shadow seemed to hang there and I saw a dark hose that could only have been blood elongate from it. The body hit the ground as I got to the switch of the desk lamp.

I was in under the desk, the flex switch in my hand but no more shots followed. I looked across at Anderson. He was in flat against the wall and gave me a thumbs-up sign. I crawled over to the window and let the plastic Venetian blind down over it. I shut the louvres to shield the room from outside and crawled back toward Anderson.

The big man in the stocking-mask was half-leaning, half-lying against the bookcase, his body held upright by the arm wedged through the shattered glass. He was still breathing but there were two holes in the front of his sweater so I didn't give him long. His pistol was lying on the carpet and I got to it and added it to my armoury.

There was no sound coming from the hallway or whatever lay beyond the room door but I could sense the presence of people outside. The lock still held and the hinges were intact but there were big holes punched through the panels.

"You'd better watch that," I told Anderson. "If you got enough ammo put a round through it from time to time."

Anderson nodded.

"I got a spare clip."

I set fire to two cigarettes, passed one over to Anderson. Then I crawled nearer the big man. I'd only got off one shot so Anderson must have hit him with the second or he'd caught crossfire from the people outside the door. He was breathing heavily, with broken, automatic snoring through the nose and dark blood was dripping through the stocking-mask. I stood up at the side of the room and ripped it off. To let him breathe more than anything else.

He had a savage-looking, Oriental face, with heavily oiled black hair. His eyes were closed and he wasn't even conscious of my presence. He took a couple more gulps of air and then found it was time to die. He sagged as I disentangled his arm and lowered him to the floor. There was something familiar about his build and the thin silk pullover he was wearing. His style was similar to the character who'd outed me on the terrace on my first visit to the house; the one I'd figured for a Korean.

I blew smoke out through my nostrils and frowned at the corpse. Then I knelt, dragged a cloth off a side table and covered the face. Bad for morale otherwise. I crawled over to Anderson, sat next him, with my back to the wall, where I could watch the windows. I got the spare Smith-Wesson rounds and reloaded. This way I could drop anyone approaching from the window end or help Anderson if anyone burst through the door. Seemed like he could read my thoughts.

"They likely to give up?" he said over his shoulder.

I shook my head.

"Not them. We'll just have to do this the hard way."

I looked moodily across at the TV set. Nothing seemed to be stirring anywhere and there was no sound from outside the house, except for the fret of the wind. I figured there'd be a lull before they tried again.

I crawled back over to the other side of the room, taking care to keep away from the area directly commanded by the door. I unplugged the flex from the set, wrapped it round the black control box and got the sheets of figures out my pocket. I made it to a divan at the side of the room, levered up the seat cushions and buried both items. Then I put the cushion back and sat on it. There was no way of detecting anything was hidden there. I sighed. It wasn't much but it was all we had for the moment.

Anderson watched me grimly.

"A bargaining counter?"

I nodded.

"Could keep us alive a little longer if it came to the point."

"You don't sound very optimistic," he said.

I shrugged.

"Just being realistic," I told him.

I put the light out again. We sat and finished the cigarettes, watching the door and window and listening to the faint sighing of the wind. Looked like being a long evening.

★ ★ ★

About an hour seemed to pass like this. When I checked I found it was all of eight minutes. Anderson was silent near me, his cigarette smoked down to a smouldering stub. He was a good man to be with in such a situation. He and the van Opper number would make an excellent team. I was glad she was pulling through. Not only for his sake. I felt better the more I thought about it. I finished off my own cigarette and leaned forward to stub it out on the floor.

My eyes were beginning to water with concentrating on the window. With the blinds down there was little light coming through. I figured they'd think twice before coming that way without being able to see inside the room. The door was the main danger. I didn't know how many Chinese hit-men were outside but however many there were, they were sure to be too many for us. I hadn't recognized Li-Fan's voice but I figured he wouldn't be far away. So much for his promises. I grinned wryly to myself in the dusk.

I turned back toward the door. I was sitting next to Anderson again now, to the right of the doorway. Several shots had shattered the panelling and I figured it needed only one charge by a determined man. With a couple through the lock they'd be on us.

Anderson moved a little closer to me.

"Why don't we get one either side the door?" he whispered. "That way we can take them from both sides."

I shook my head.

"Too dangerous. We're more likely to fire into each other that way, especially in this light."

Anderson's face creased up in a grin.

"That's what makes you the pro, Mr Faraday."

"There's too many imponderables in a set-up like this," I said. "Why lengthen the odds?"

I put my hand on his shoulder. My ears had caught a faint rustling outside the window. At the same time there was a noise in the hall like the padding of feet.

"Get back in the corner," I said.

I stayed up near the door. Two shots came through it, the sounds like a physical blow in the heavy silence. Splinters of wood flew about the room and acrid blue smoke poured in through the hole. I was just bringing the Smith-Wesson up when the window blinds burst open. Gold flame licked along the floor, made the interior of the room a lurid furnace.

I saw Anderson snaking away behind a bureau, holding his pistol out, searching for a target. The bottle of blazing petrol shattered against the wall near me and ricochetted back into the centre of the room. I felt my clothes beginning to burn as two dark figures burst in the remains of the door.

I got the nearest in the leg and he spun off into the flames, his screams rising to a high pitch as his clothing caught fire. The second, bigger figure turned on his heel, the tommy-gun up high, flames glinting on the barrel. Anderson shot him through the mouth while he was correcting his aim. The sub-machine gun went skittering into the pyre in the middle of the room as its owner slammed backward to the far wall where he remained pinned for a long second before sliding to the floor, leaving a scarlet trail on the wall behind him. The shells started exploding in the heat, adding to the charm of the evening.

Other figures were smashing in the window now, advancing through the flames. I got off three shots, wriggled aside, beating at my burning coat. The entire room seemed filled with smoke and the heavy reverberations. Anderson was flat in against the far wall, making a small target. The men round the window were too close; they were jammed into a comparatively cramped space and confused by the unfamiliarity of the room, the shifting glare of the fire and the heavy smoke which partly obscured the surroundings.

The nearest shot vaguely toward the door, succeeded in stitching a Eurasian who was just bursting in. He turned away, clutching his stomach. A small, wiry figure with a soulless yellow face came out the flames like a demon king from a childhood pantomime. The eyes glistened behind the rubber mask. I waited until he was almost up to me before I gave him the last slug in the belly. He was suddenly hinged in the middle, coming down, the long knife in his hand bouncing away on the burning floor. His head hit the wall near me and left a dark smear on it.

I clubbed at him with the Smith-Wesson but there was no need. Long driblets of blood oozed out the mouthpiece as I tore at the mask. It came away in my hand, revealing a bland yellow face, the eyes already glazing in death. I didn't waste any time in sympathy. I was already stuffing fresh shells into the Smith-Wesson. The flames grew before my eyes, blurring the room. I couldn't see Anderson now. I was choking with the heavy black smoke, my senses going. I reached out for the wall, grateful for its solidity.

The figures had faded and there was an enormous quiet, broken only by a tearing noise which must have been the crackling of the flames. I sat and fought to keep my senses while the burning room buckled and reeled about me. I was still hanging on to the rim of consciousness when I heard faint sounds like slamming doors coming from the night outside.

There were running footsteps in the darkness and shouts. I must have passed out for a minute or two. When I came to myself again water was flooding into the room. I raised the Smith-Wesson, suddenly aware it was no longer in my hand. I fought to focus my eyes, saw Anderson was being helped to his feet by a tall Chinese. He dragged him out the room. Strong arms caught me underneath the armpits; my heels grated on the floor as I was lifted backwards into the hall. There were many feet running to and fro.

I sat in a corner of the hallway looking at Anderson's smoke-streaked face and streaming eyes. I retched for a bit, found I could breathe again. The flames seemed to be under control now but the buckets were still coming.

Some legs came into focus. They were very elegant legs, composed of immaculate lightweight grey suiting. They terminated in very expensive-looking crocodile skin shoes. I dragged my eyes upward, met the concerned gaze of Li-Fan.

He inclined his head with an ironic smile, looking from me to the half-conscious figure of Anderson.

"I seem to have come just in time, Mr Faraday," he said politely.

20

"You can say that again," I said.

My voice came out my mouth in a withered croak. Li-Fan bent toward me, proffering the Smith-Wesson butt first.

"We thought it best to relieve you of it, Mr Faraday. Just in case of any unfortunate mistakes."

"You were wise," I said. "Most Orientals look alike to Western eyes. Especially when coming through smoke."

The tall man chuckled. He glanced round at the shattered door of the room we'd just left, from which fumes were still pouring.

"I trust you did not think I or my men were responsible for this crude and brutal charade?"

"You have a delicate way of putting it," I said. "Frankly, I didn't know what to think."

Li-Fan shook his head. There was a note of asperity in his voice as he replied.

"I have tried to put you on the right path, Mr Faraday, but old habits die hard."

He glanced over at Anderson.

"Your friend is all right. Just overcome by smoke."

He fished in the pocket of his elegant suit and came up with a gold cigarette case.

"You don't mind if I smoke?"

I grinned.

"It would hardly make any difference."

He extended the case to me. I waved it away.

"I've had enough for one evening."

I got up, found I could stand. Li-Fan watched me with expressionless eyes. I put the Smith-Wesson back in the holster, went over to help Anderson up. His eyes were red-rimmed and weeping, his face pale but otherwise he seemed all right.

"Let us go in here. My men have the fire under control."

Li-Fan led the way into an elegant room on the other side of the hall. He buttoned the light-switch and the

236

overhead fixture shimmered down on a bar with glass-fitted shelves and rows of bottles.

"I think a drink would be in order."

"Make mine a Scotch," I said. "Straight."

Anderson put his pistol in an inner pocket of his jacket.

"I'll go along with that," he said steadily.

His eyes were asking me all sorts of questions but I held off. I waited for the Chinese to make the opening. The tramping feet of his men were still coming and going through the house. I saw the body of one of the Chinese from the far room being carried past.

"What are you going to do with them?" I said.

Li-Fan smiled. He came back from the bar with two glasses in which ice chinked.

"There are funeral-parlours in Chinatown where everything making for proper form will be carried out and no questions asked."

"Convenient," I said.

Li-Fan's eyes were wide and bland.

"You would prefer to remain and explain to the police?"

I raised my glass in salute.

"You've got me there. We'll leave things as they stand."

"Very wise, Mr Faraday. To you and your friend."

"This is Quincey Anderson," I said. "He's engaged to the young lady who was seriously wounded when Greenbach got dead. He's been a lot of help tonight."

Li-Fan looked at Anderson with respect on his face.

"A special salute, Mr Anderson. You gave an excellent account of yourself."

"How did you get out here?" I said.

Li-Fan looked pained.

"Mr Faraday, you have never been out of our sight for one moment. As I said, we have a large organization."

I gave him a long, hard look.

"Now the social chitchat's over," I said. "Let's get down to cases."

Li-Fan shrugged. With his pale skin, athletic build and thick black hair he looked even younger than when I'd last seen him.

"We want the black box, of course."

I took another sip of whisky, feeling energy beginning to flood back into me.

"Supposing I won't give it up?"

Li-Fan shifted one of his elegantly shod feet, glancing casually from myself to Anderson and then back again.

"My dear Mr Faraday, I am sure you would never do anything so foolish."

"I'm not in much of a position to argue," I said. "And you did save my life, for which I'm not ungrateful. For the second time, incidentally. But I'd like to know more about the use to which it's to be put. The black box, I mean."

Li-Fan sipped at the whisky appreciatively.

"Oh, I don't think you'd quarrel with that, Mr Faraday. I'm going to use it to waste Jimmy Chan."

I stared at him blankly.

"Jimmy Chan?"

Li-Fan stared back at me unwinkingly.

"Naturally, Mr Faraday. Mr Wong's nephew."

★ ★ ★

239

I went on swapping glances with Li-Fan. He didn't waver or drop his eyes a fraction. The fire was out now and the house was filled with the harsh, acrid stench of charred woodwork and fabric.

"Supposing I bought it, Li-Fan?"

Again the irritation on the smooth, cultured face.

"It doesn't matter whether you buy it or not, Mr Faraday. I am speaking the truth."

"I thought you said you didn't go in for violence," I said.

Li-Fan smiled thinly.

"We would bring in outside help, Mr Faraday."

"A professional hit-man?" I said.

Li-Fan raised his eyebrows.

"We are legitimate businessmen. We do not waste people ourselves."

"A highly ethical point," I told him.

Li-Fan held up his hand, his face suddenly grave.

"You do not understand, Mr Faraday. I would like to show you something. Can you spare the time?"

I looked at him for a long moment.

"I have all the time in the world now, thanks to you."

Li-Fan's features relaxed.

"You are a sensible man, Mr Faraday. And now, the black box, if you please. We shall need it to transmit our own messages."

I nodded.

"To bring the distributors together?"

"Something like that, Mr Faraday."

"All right," I said. "I'll buy it."

I went back into the charred wreckage of the room we'd just left. I crossed to the divan and rummaged around in the cushions. I came back and gave the transmitting device to Li-Fan. He looked at it incuriously.

"The formula, if you please."

"You have it there," I said.

The tall Chinese unrolled the paper from round the flex. He studied it for a moment, then got out his gold lighter. Anderson watched stupefied as he set light to the documents. He dropped them on the floor and waited until they had been reduced to ashes. He ground them thoughtfully into powder with the sole of one elegant shoe.

"I don't get it," I said.

Li-Fan pursed his lips.

"This is something the world can do without," he said gently.

It took me a few seconds to find my voice.

"You aren't working with Mr Wong?" I said.

Li-Fan bowed slightly.

"Allow me to congratulate you on your reasoning prowess," he said ironically. "I am working for Mr Wong. There is a world of difference. We do not always see eye to eye."

"Supposing he finds out?" I said.

Li-Fan shook his head.

"He won't," he said. "Why do you think I sent my men away? And you won't tell him."

"How can you be sure of that?" I said.

"By reading your character, Mr Faraday. I am seldom wrong in such matters. You share my own abhorrence of the horrors of drug-trafficking."

"But you're mixed up in it yourself," I said.

Li-Fan shook his head. A shadow passed across his face.

"As I have already told you to the point of nausea, I am a business man. I handle Mr Wong's legitimate commercial enterprises. He has a vast empire. Even I do not know the extent of it. I control only legal, highly reputable companies."

I stared at him for a long moment.

"There's a good deal to you, Li-Fan. What makes you care whether I believe you or not?"

"I care, Mr Faraday. Let us leave it at that. When you have been home with me and seen what I wish to show you, you will understand better."

I nodded.

"Wong will kill you if he finds out what you've done."

"I think not, Mr Faraday. In the first place, he is not going to find out. Secondly, I am going to use this black box to smash the ring. Thirdly, he will not find that out either. Fourthly, I am going to waste his nephew in the process.

That he approves of. Chan will get the blame for everything, including the loss of the black box."

He shrugged.

"He always does. And you will have achieved your purpose, Mr Faraday. But for me you would certainly never have succeeded."

"Sounds fine," I said. "I have no choice anyway."

Li-Fan smiled a sincere smile.

"You certainly have not, Mr Faraday."

"What are you going to do with the black box?"

"When I have extracted its information, destroy it."

Li-Fan glanced toward the window.

"After all, if it had fallen into your hands it would have been all the same. Another clever Dr Greenbach would only have arisen and invented something similar. By destroying it we are merely delaying the spread of an evil. Drug-trafficking can only be controlled by governments. And as they are nearly all corrupt, there is no will there."

"You're quite a philosopher," I said.

Li-Fan smiled for the last time, looking across the hall toward the wreckage of the shattered room.

"There has been enough talking, Mr Faraday. If your companion is ready we will make a start."

21

Li-Fan pulled the big black Caddy smoothly up the gravel drive, stopped in front of a white-painted three-car garage and killed the motor. Anderson drew the Buick in behind us and sat waiting, his face a blank mask. I got out the passenger seat and walked back to him.

"Best wait here," I said. "I shan't be long."

Anderson nodded.

"Will do."

Li-Fan was beside me now. He guided me courteously up a zig-zag cement path that wound between smooth turf and on to a gracious colonnaded terrace. I couldn't see much of the house because it was dark and there were few lights in the windows, except for a couple in the top storey. The wind sighed heavily in the tree-tops and seemed to make the atmosphere oppressive.

"Quite a spread," I said.

"We like it," Li-Fan said deprecatingly.

He opened the big front door, using a key he took from his pocket. We were in a vast hall with a white-painted staircase winding up to the right. All the light came from the area at the top of the stairs, leaving the ground-floor in darkness. I suddenly felt very tired. It had been a long night and it wasn't half over yet.

A tall Chinese woman of about thirty-five to forty, strikingly beautiful, in a white silk gown with a high-button collar came down the staircase with lithe, effortless movements. Her sad eyes searched Li-Fan's face. He introduced me.

"This is my wife, Mr Faraday."

I mumbled something appropriate but the tall woman acknowledged my presence without speaking, merely making a gracious inclination of her head. She answered Li-Fan's unspoken question in a low, well-modulated voice.

"No change."

A heavy sigh escaped Li-Fan's lips, despite his habitual reserve and his wife rested her hand very gently on his forearm for a brief moment.

"This way, Mr Faraday."

Li-Fan moved forward across the hall and beckoned me up the stairs. On the landing at the top corridors stretched off in three directions. There was the hushed atmosphere of a sick-room. The Chinese indicated an oak door in front of us.

"If you would like to wash up, you will find everything you require in there."

I suddenly realized that my hands and probably my face were blackened with smoke and streaked with grime. I must have been quite a spectacle to Li-Fan's wife. Her reception of me was a tribute to her good manners though there was obviously something badly wrong in the house. I could sense that a mile off. I thanked the Chinese and went on into an elegant cloakroom. I ignored the blackened scarecrow in the mirror and scrubbed up.

When I'd finished I passed a comb through my hair, re-knotted my tie and found I was almost presentable enough for a Rotary dinner. Providing I was sitting in a dark corner. When I came out Li-Fan was still standing in the same position on the landing as though he'd solidified there. He led me forward down the corridor and opened up a door on the right.

A white-coated nurse appeared in the opening; there was a warning in her eyes. The room was dimly lit, the available lighting coming from shaded lamps tilted up to favour the ceiling. There were screens in one corner and a slender Chinese in a white coat doing something with a basin. Instruments and equipment glittered dully in the indistinct lighting. I could hear a faint moaning noise now and the hair began to rise on my scalp.

Li-Fan put his hand on my arm with a reassuring pressure.

"This is not very pretty, Mr Faraday, but I want you to be sure of my motives."

"I'm ready," I said.

We walked round the screen. Another nurse moved away as we drew near the bed. Lying on it was the remains of a once handsome young Chinese. He was about eighteen years old and would have been fine once. His face was a mask of perspiration which ran down his hollow cheeks. He jerked and writhed on the bed and I noticed there were heavy straps across the coverlets.

Moaning noises came out his mouth, together with driblets of spittle. His lips were contorted in a permanent rictus and his convulsive struggles to escape the straps gave the impression of a galvanic strength behind the frail build.

His arms were covered with bandages soaked with blood and pus and as I watched, the nurse who'd opened the door came swiftly back to change one of the dressings. There was an intravenous drip connected to his left arm but his latest struggles had torn it out the vein and the nurse swiftly reinserted it. I know what Li-Fan was going to say before he opened his mouth.

"My only son. His life and his parents' completely ruined by drugs. Unknown to us he was a runner for Jimmy Chan's organization."

"I'm sorry," I said and meant it.

Li-Fan slowly shook his head.

"There's no need to be," he said

gently. "It is not your fault. But you can now see why the black box will be safe in my keeping."

I stood looking down at the boy, a thousand thoughts chasing themselves through what was left of my mind.

"He has only a short time to go," said Li-Fan softly. "He will be dead within three days."

I opened my mouth to speak but Li-Fan stopped me by putting his hand on my arm.

"It is all right. He cannot hear us."

He looked down at the boy's contorted face. The second nurse had come round and was sponging away the perspiration now.

"He is beyond us. He has been dead a long time."

"So you were using me?" I said.

Li-Fan nodded slowly.

"You could say that, Mr Faraday. But not in any sordid sense. One uses the instrument to hand. And you were a very powerful instrument for my purposes."

"Glad to have been of service," I said.

Li-Fan looked at me almost absently, turning up his eyes from the bed where the exhausted figure of his son was acting out the last few hours of his short life.

"A quiet room in hell," I said.

Li-Fan shrugged.

"You may well say so, Mr Faraday."

I went on out and left him there in the quietness and the pain, the only sound the faint mechanical moans that might have been made by the wind. I was glad to reach the outside air.

* * *

I dropped Anderson off at Zelda van Opper's apartment. It was plenty late now but I had some unfinished business that couldn't wait until morning. It started to rain again as I drove across town and by the time I got to the Clairmont Apartments it was coming down a treat. Della Strongman lived at No. 34. It was a pretty plushy place and by the time I'd fought my way up to the third floor I was knee-deep in custom-built carpeting.

It was around half-two in the morning

but it seemed like three weeks since I'd left Stella at the office the previous afternoon to pick up the Buick. But that's how it happened sometimes. I found 34 and hit the button. I didn't expect Della Strongman to be up at that time of the morning, but to my surprise the door was opened on a chain almost immediately. Della Strongman's eyes were wide and surprised.

"Mike!"

"What's left of him," I said. "I know it's the wrong hour but can I come in?"

"Sure. Why not?"

She slid the chain back and held the door wide. She wore a white and blue striped dressing gown and she looked as fresh as though it were two-thirty in the afternoon. A record player was softly spraying a Mozart horn-piece or something about that price-range into the silence. She slipped the door to behind me and locked it. She glanced at me appraisingly.

"You look a little worse for wear, Mike."

"You can say that again," I told her.

"The whole case just blew wide open."

The eyes opened in surprise but she said nothing.

"You're up late," I said.

The face was frank and open like always.

"I couldn't sleep, Mike. It happens sometimes. So I fixed myself a glass of milk and a sandwich. Can I get you something?"

"I wouldn't say no to a pint of hot coffee," I said.

She motioned me to a deep leather armchair and went up some marble steps at the side of the room that presumably led to the kitchen area. The apartment was open-plan with lots of white walls and indoor greenery; anyway it was pretty nice and any other time it would have been great. But not tonight. And not under these circumstances.

I sat back and let the Mozart horns sift effortlessly through my brain. In among the rhythmic procession of notes came a succession of dollar signs. I grinned. There had been something at the back of my mind for the past hour or so. It was Mr Wong's ten thousand dollars. I likely wouldn't be seeing it now.

I hoped his people wouldn't come after me to make sure I kept my end of the bargain. In all the shambles out at Greenbach's place I'd forgotten to discuss it with Li-Fan. But I guessed he'd make it all right with Wong. He'd have to do that if he wanted to waste the Chan character. And to achieve it he had to have an out for me. Anyway, if I didn't hear any more from Wong within the next twenty-four hours I knew I'd never hear from him. I gave up beating my brains out and sat back and listened to the music.

It finished and the machine switched off. I opened my eyes. It was then I saw the white fox fur heaped carelessly up at one end of a long leather divan. I had another image of the same fur or its identical twin in Dillon's apartment. It was another Bad Sight of the Month to go with all the detritus that was lodging like grit at the back of my mind.

The girl had returned now, carrying a tray down the short flight of steps. She put it down on a low table near my chair and poured the coffee with a steady hand.

"So the case blew up, Mike?"

I nodded.

"I wondered when you were going to ask."

Della Strongman went on pouring her own coffee and carried my cup over. I put both hands round the beaker, savouring the hot, steamy fragrance in my nostrils I sat back, shut my eyes and got the first sips down me. I could feel energy flowing back. I opened my eyes again.

The girl sat on the divan opposite me, held her own cup and watched me without saying anything. I finished the coffee, got up for a re-fill.

"You don't seem very curious," I said.

"You'll tell me when you're ready, Mike," she said.

"I'm ready now," I told her. "Greenbach was in a drugs racket up to his eyeballs. He'd found out a new method of refining the stuff and he used TV to transmit details of the drops to his organization."

Della Strongman's eyes opened wide. The lamplight glistened on her blonde hair as her eyes searched my face.

"Sounds fantastic, Mike."

"Doesn't it?" I said. "I nearly got my head blown off tonight. Seems I mixed in a hassle between Greenbach's set-up and a Chinese Triad group."

The girl's face had a half-frozen look.

"What are you trying to tell me, Mike?"

"You gave me a phoney steer about a new method of refining gasoline," I said.

Della Strongman's eyes flashed.

"I told you the truth, Mike. Those were the papers I saw on Dillon's desk. You don't think I had anything to do with this?"

I put down my coffee cup.

"I don't know what to think, honey. That fox fur, for instance. I saw that in Dillon's apartment the last time I was there."

The girl's eyes were dancing with amusement.

"If we weren't almost strangers I'd say you were jealous."

"This is too important to joke about," I said.

The girl licked her lips. She put down her coffee cup.

"If we go on like this, Mike, we'll both say something we'll be sorry for. There's only one way to settle it."

I nodded.

"It's pretty late but we've got to do it tonight."

Della Strongman stood up. She looked even taller than I'd remembered.

"I'll go get dressed."

22

It was still raining when I tooled the Buick into the courtyard of Dillon's apartment block. There were lights on in his windows. The girl sat at my side in a white raincoat with a pale blue scarf at the throat and looked thoughtful. I got out and slammed the door. The girl followed my glance up to the window.

"He keeps late hours," she said.

"You don't seem surprised," I said.

Della Strongman shrugged.

"Should I be?"

"You tell me. Dillon wouldn't be asleep tonight. Not after what's happened."

"You haven't told me what happened, Mike."

"We'll go into that later," I said.

We walked up and I hit the button of Dillon's apartment. It took him a long time to answer. When he did he was fully dressed in a lightweight grey suit and immaculate silk tie. His jaw dropped when he saw me. I shoved past him, the girl following in behind. There were a lot of suitcases strewn around and other signs of packing.

"Going somewhere?" I said.

Dillon's eyes showed white. He'd lost all his old steely manner.

"A case out of town," he said.

"I'll bet," I told him.

He moved round behind the lid of an open suitcase. I stepped over and chopped his wrist with the edge of my hand. He gave a yelp of pain. The little blued-steel automatic bounced to the carpet. I put my foot on it. Dillon's face turned green.

"Why did you do that, Mr Faraday?"

"Just normal routine with me," I said. "I don't like to have guns pointed at me. And there have been too many pointed at me tonight."

I avoided looking at the girl, raked my eyes round the apartment. The drapes at the window were moving slightly though there was no air in the room.

"Get over to the door," I told the girl. "Lock it and throw me the key."

She smiled.

"You trusting me all of a sudden?"

"Maybe. We'll see after you've given me the key."

"What the hell is this?" Dillon said quickly. "And what is Miss Strongman doing here this time of the morning?"

"Just slumming," I said.

I picked up Dillon's pistol and watched while the Strongman number went over to the door. She locked it and threw me the key like I'd asked her.

"Just try the door," I said.

The girl smiled lazily.

"You don't trust anyone do you?"

"That's why I stay in one piece," I said.

Dillon moved away from the suitcase. I threw off the safety of the automatic and waved it in his direction.

"Don't try anything fancy. Just sit down so we can have a nice little talk."

Dillon's face changed from green to off-white. He would have made a great traffic signal. His eyes flickered to the rear of the room. He went over and sat on the edge of a ladder-back chair near the wall.

"I suppose there must be a reason for this outrage?" he said.

I turned back to the girl.

"Try the door."

She turned the handle, tugged at it. She was smiling as she came back down the room.

I looked at Dillon thoughtfully. He stared sullenly at the carpet as though he'd been caught out rigging a jury. With his style it wouldn't have been the first time.

"You set me up," I said.

Dillon flushed. He tried the bright legal smile but it faded as quickly as it appeared on his face.

"What the hell are you talking about, Faraday?"

"You know what I'm talking about," I said. "You left those documents on the gasoline crap around for Miss Strongman to find. That was one of your ways of putting people off the scent."

Dillon half got up from the chair.

"If only you'd . . . "

I waved him back down with the pistol barrel.

"Just stay put until I've finished. You rubbed Greenbach yourself. Why split with him when you could grab the whole operation for yourself?"

Dillon's face had turned an ashen colour. Driblets of spittle ran out the corner of his mouth.

"You must be mad, Faraday."

I shook my head.

"Not mad. Just wising up, though it took me long enough."

I looked at the girl. Her breath was coming hard and fast as she glanced from me to her employer.

"But the Triads muscling in scared you. You daren't go to the police. So you hired me. Me protecting Greenbach was a blind. He was due to get rubbed anyway. But my presence on the case provided an alibi for you. If I rubbed a few Triads, so much the better. That way you could go on skimming off the cream because no-one knew you were connected with the racket. Conversely, if I got the chop that strengthened your position as Greenbach's protector."

I smiled at the girl.

"Greenbach wasn't frightened of the Triads. He took no precautions. But you were afraid his premature death might involve you. When you were certain he had no documents linking you, you had him wasted. That was you ringing the other night at the Laurel Canyon house, wasn't it? Making sure your hit-man had done his job properly? Only I was already there."

Dillon's face had sagged, leaving him looking old and haggard.

"Going to find this pretty difficult to prove, aren't you?" he sneered.

"I don't think so," I said. "Particularly when I produce the hit-man."

I got the two shots off so quickly they seemed like one. Powder-smoke stung my cheeks. The drapes at the far end of the room billowed as two holes were punched in them. Something big and bulky came forward, tearing the curtaining from the hooks. The big man in the dark suit was already dead but he didn't know it. He took another three steps, the scarlet stains spreading on his white shirt-front. His cannon hit the carpeting a fraction before he did.

★ ★ ★

The smoke had hardly time to reach the ceiling before sound came back. I could hear traffic noises above the roaring in my ears. Dillon had sunk over the arm of his chair, making retching noises in his throat. The girl tried a bright smile, couldn't quite make it.

"There's some liquor in the cabinet over there," I said. "Pour us some stiff ones."

I went over to the big man's body, ignoring the lawyer. The former couldn't have been any deader. I studied him curiously. I didn't know him. I came back to Dillon, waited until Della Strongman brought the drinks. The rye seemed to bring back some of the colour to her cheeks. I waited while Dillon emptied his glass and poured another.

"There's your hit-man," I said. "Shouldn't be too difficult to tie you in."

Dillon shook his head dully.

"I'm not saying anything," he said. "It's my right. Not until I see a lawyer."

I grinned.

"Bring him a mirror," I told the girl.

She came and put a warm hand on my shoulder. Her fingers trembled very slightly as she poured me another drink.

I set fire to a cigarette and stood listening to the faint traffic noises outside the window. That was when I saw the white fox-fur lying on a chair up near the drapes. I glanced at the girl. She pulled down the corner of her mouth with a wry expression and I knew then she'd seen it too.

"If it's any good I'd say I'm sorry," I told her.

She shrugged.

"You might try."

"I'm sorry," I said.

She raised her glass in a small gesture of salutation. I turned back to Dillon. He had his head in his hands this time.

"If you've nothing further to add we'll be going down-town," I said.

He got up, looking vaguely about him

266

like he'd lost a case in court. The grey suit seemed to sag on him now, as if it was two sizes too big. The flinty grey eyes looked crushed and defeated and the fleshy mouth had fallen in over the white teeth like he was an old man.

He shrugged with something of his old manner, draining the whisky in the bottom of his glass.

"Why not?"

I waited while he collected his raincoat. I put the pistol back in my pocket. Della Strongman unlocked the door and followed us out. We walked down the corridor to the elevator. Dillon buttoned it in silence. It seemed like a long time before it came up. The door slid open and we got in. We glided down toward the ground floor. The girl hit the switch that operated the door. She stood still, surprise on her face. Dillon stepped out, triumph in his eyes. I followed him, reaching for the Smith-Wesson. I stopped. The girl standing in the doorway facing me smiled faintly.

"Just hold it there, Mr Faraday," she said.

She held the pistol rock-steady on my gut.

"Well, well," I said. "Little Miss Muffet."

Dillon went round in rear of me, got his pistol and my Smith-Wesson. He broke the Smith-Wesson, spilling the shells on the floor of the elevator. He flung the weapon after it. He stood for a moment and then struck me across the face with the barrel of his own pistol. I felt blood trickle down my face.

"I bet you do that to all your clients," I said.

I looked thoughtfully at the girl. She had the white fox-fur draped casually over one shoulder.

"I should have known," I said.

Miss Popkiss smiled, showing beautiful teeth.

"You remember me then, Mr Faraday?"

"How could I forget you?" I said. "You work at the oil company offices, on the floor below Dillon."

She nodded, passing a tongue across very full lips. She still wore the blue linen shirt, or one very like it and the pale blue slacks that set off the boyish slimness of her figure. Her dark hair shimmered under the overhead light as she moved casually, her body a well-disciplined instrument.

"You must be pretty fit," I said.

"I can run down three flights easily enough, Mr Faraday," she said calmly, keeping her eyes on me, not looking at Della Strongman.

"I was in the bedroom and heard everything."

"I bet you did," I said. "What now?"

"In the elevator," Dillon said, gesturing jerkily with the pistol. He looked less in control of himself than the Popkiss number so I did as he said. Della Strongman followed me in, saying nothing. Dillon smiled briefly as the elevator door closed. We whined upward for perhaps thirty seconds. Then the cage jerked to a stop as the lights went out.

"What happened?" Della Strongman whispered.

"Guess the girl got to the power switch," I said.

We waited, hearing the retreating

footsteps down below. Then a car gunned up in front of the apartments and whispered away into the night.

"Sorry I couldn't do anything, Mike," the girl said.

"Glad you didn't," I said. "There have been enough stiffs lying around so far."

I laughed, reaching for my handkerchief and cleaning up my face. A little light was coming into the elevator cage now; just enough for me to make out Della Strongman's expression.

"Let them run," I said. "They won't get very far."

Della Strongman came over and put warm fingers on my face, the tips tracing out the line of my jaw.

"We might be here for hours, Mike," she whispered.

"Who's complaining?" I said.

She was already unbuttoning her raincoat as she came into my arms.

23

"Coffee?" Stella said.

"Try me," I told her.

A fine mist was coming down on the boulevard outside and through the rain I could see the shimmer on the body-work of the stalled automobiles. I sat back at my old broad-top and studied that morning's *Examiner*. There was a front-page spread on the Triad massacre.

"They wasted Jimmy Chan all right," Stella said, popping her head round the glass screen.

"In spades," I said.

"You think Li-Fan will keep his word, Mike?"

"He already has," I told her.

Stella shook the gold bell of her hair impatiently.

"I mean about the drug-ring and destroying the black box."

I looked moodily across to where the plastic-bladed fan pecked at the frayed edges of the silence.

"He was serious," I said. "If you'd seen his son . . . "

Stella bit her lip, her very blue eyes fixed on my face. She was about to reply when the phone buzzed.

She went over to her own desk and sat down behind her typewriter.

"Faraday Investigations."

She frowned across at me.

"Oh, yes, Lieutenant. He went out about half an hour ago but I'm expecting him back this afternoon. Yes, I'll tell him."

She put the receiver back with a broad smile.

"That was the police, as if you didn't know. They want you down at City Hall day after tomorrow."

"I'll be there," I said.

Stella went back to the alcove and busied herself with cups and saucers. The aroma of the coffee set me salivating. I looked at myself in the telephone mirror. I was almost as good as new. I grinned and flipped it back in the tray beneath the instrument.

Stella came back and put the cup down on my blotter, reached over the sugar basin. She fetched her own cup and sat on the edge of my desk, swinging a long leg and looking at me in that disconcerting manner of hers.

"I forgot to tell you," she said. "Della Strongman rang in before you arrived. She said she'd meet you tonight at eight o'clock. She said you'd know the place."

"Sure," I said. "It's about a new job I'm trying to get for her."

Stella didn't actually laugh but her eyes looked like she was laughing inside.

"That'll be the day," she said darkly.

I sat and finished my coffee, raking around in the biscuit tin for my nut fudge favourite, not thinking about anything in particular. I studied the headlines in the paper again. There was another bulletin on the van Opper number. She was off the danger list.

"You sent those roses?" I asked.

Stella nodded.

"Sure," she said. "A dozen, like you wanted. Anderson said they were both expecting you over at the hospital this afternoon. She can talk now."

I nodded.

"Let's shut up shop early and both go."

"Fine," Stella said. "If you think the budget can stand it."

"It can stand it," I said.

Stella stopped swinging her leg and went back to her own desk.

"How much do you think Dillon will draw, Mike?"

"About ten to fifteen if he's lucky," I said. "He's got a good lawyer."

Stella gave me a long look.

"How did you know they'd make for the Mex border?"

"I could say intuition," I told her. "But I'd be lying. Della Strongman told me he had business interests and money in a safe deposit in Mexico City. He and the girl had to go there before they ran out of funds."

Stella nodded.

"Funny thing about her. Do you think they'll find her?"

I grinned.

"Maybe. Maybe not. She's not important. About the only decent thing Dillon ever did was in helping her to disappear. Human nature's a strange business."

"You can say that again, Mike."

I opened the big manilla envelope for the second time, looked at the fat stack of C-notes. There was no message with the money but there didn't have to be. The bills added up to ten thousand dollars exactly.

"Li-Fan's a man of his word," Stella said softly. "You want me to deposit these?"

I shook my head.

"I'm surely tempted but I don't like their source. We'll try and off-load these on to an anti-drugs rehabilitation programme."

"I thought you said Li-Fan's business enterprises were legitimate."

"So they are," I said. "But this money came from Wong. And two Wongs don't make a Wight in my book."

Stella winced, looking at me with little lights dancing in her eyes.

"I bet you waited all the case to get that one out," she said. "And in any event that joke went out with Coolidge."

"It nearly went out with me," I said.

There didn't seem anything else to say so I went on out as well. Stella was still smiling as I got to the door.

THE END

NIGHT FROST
THE LONELY PLACE
CRACK IN THE SIDEWALK
IMPACT
THE DARK MIRROR
NO LETTERS FROM THE GRAVE
THE MARBLE ORCHARD
A VOICE FROM THE DEAD

Other titles in the Linford Mystery Library:

A GENTEEL LITTLE MURDER
Philip Daniels

Gilbert had a long-cherished plan to murder his wife. When the polished Edward entered the scene Gilbert's attitude was suddenly changed.

DEATH AT THE WEDDING
Madelaine Duke

Dr. Norah North's search for a killer takes her from a wedding to a private hospital.

MURDER FIRST CLASS
Ron Ellis

Will Detective Chief Inspector Glass find the Post Office robbers before the Executioner gets to them?

A FOOT IN THE GRAVE
Bruce Marshall

About to be imprisoned and tortured in Buenos Aires, John Smith escapes, only to become involved in an aeroplane hijacking.

DEAD TROUBLE
Martin Carroll

Trespassing brought Jennifer Denning more than she bargained for. She was totally unprepared for the violence which was to lie in her path.

HOURS TO KILL
Ursula Curtiss

Margaret went to New Mexico to look after her sick sister's rented house and felt a sharp edge of fear when the absent landlady arrived.

THE DEATH OF ABBE DIDIER
Richard Grayson

Inspector Gautier of the Sûreté investigates three crimes which are strangely connected.

NIGHTMARE TIME
Hugh Pentecost

Have the missing major and his wife met with foul play somewhere in the Beaumont Hotel, or is their disappearance a carefully planned step in an act of treason?

BLOOD WILL OUT
Margaret Carr

Why was the manor house so oddly familiar to Elinor Howard? Who would have guessed that a Sunday School outing could lead to murder?

THE DRACULA MURDERS
Philip Daniels

The Horror Ball was interrupted by a spectral figure who warned the merrymakers they were tampering

THE LADIES
OF LAMBTON GREEN
Liza Shepherd

Why did murdered Robin Colquhoun's picture pose such a threat to the ladies of Lambton Green?

CARNABY
AND THE GAOLBREAKERS
Peter N. Walker

Detective Sergeant James Aloysius Carnaby-King is sent to prison as bait. When he joins in an escape he is thrown headfirst into a vicious murder hunt.